THE
CTZ
PARADIGM

THE
CTZ
PARADIGM

YVES REGIS FRANCOIS

DOUBLEDAY & COMPANY, INC.

GARDEN CITY, NEW YORK

1975

All of the characters in this book are fictitious, and any resemblance to actual persons, living or dead, is purely coincidental.

First Edition

ISBN: 0-385-07745-9
Library of Congress Catalog Card Number 74–17769
Copyright © 1975 by Yves Barbero
All Rights Reserved
Printed in the United States of America

Maggie Newman and
Benjamin Nelson
. . . true teachers

THE
CTZ
PARADIGM

PRELUDE

CELEBRATION

It was a lumbering creature which had spotted Mistress Liennie. Her 135 pounds would be no match for its eight tons.

In Liennie's hand was a two-ounce weapon. It would make up for the difference.

The slim weapon, set correctly, was not deadly to the prehistoric herbivore approaching Mistress Liennie. There was even a possibility that the creature's poor concentration, exceeded only by its poor eyesight, would forget the small human.

Liennie hoped for that. If the creature attacked, it would be in error. Liennie would not be a source of food the creature could use.

Liennie was an alien. Her daisy chain of protein would be of no use to it. Besides, the mammal was considered a friend to the human settlers. Its prime source of food was man's deadliest enemy on the planet.

If necessary, she would render it unconscious. She hoped she wouldn't have to. It was not her purpose to interfere with it.

The creature did not forget her. It approached slowly, with purpose. Soon, it passed the imaginary line she had drawn.

She fired between its poor eyes.

It sank on the sand. It would be out for half a Hobar day—eighteen hours, Terran.

She moved toward it and stroked its huge head. That was a gesture. The creature had no sensitivity which could be felt with less than the blow of a sledgehammer.

Almost ritualistically, she apologized softly. She unstrapped her belt pack and drew a needle which she stuck in a vein. The contents would supply the animal with enough food while it slept.

She moved on. Her journey had only been a Hobarian day long. Two more were needed.

The winds were increasing.

The nightly storm was nearly upon her. The temperature dropped twenty degrees in an instant.

No human would survive the next hour unprotected.

Hobar was daily reminding the human settlers that it was not designed for them.

Liennie stopped and drew her pack from the belt. From it, she took four six-inch rods. She placed them in a square six feet by eight and took control. She pressed the combination suited to the condition.

The rods came alive and stood, each extending three feet below the sand and seven feet above. The field came on; a dull blue cube was created.

She set the control for seventy degrees. The field would protect her for the next fifteen hours, making her comfortable, filtering through the necessary air and keeping her warm. It would block out the wind, its howling voice, its deadly speed.

She sat cross-legged and used the ancient meditation.

Thoughts came. She drove them out. The thoughts changed to images. She drove them out too.

There was a slight floating sensation. The cube was adjusting itself. It would rise as the sand tried to bury it. All automatically.

After a time, she slept.

Morning came, she knew. Her eyes opened. The dull blue cube was tinged by the severe sun, but the dial on her control did not indicate safety. The wind was still strong.

More meditation, a different sort, to revive her thoughts, her imagery.

An hour later, safety. She broke the cube.

There was violence all around her. Huge dunes, caused by the previous night's storm and high winds, showed it. Life that was now lifeless.

She had been spared a spring storm.

Liennie lifted a Hobarian insect, two pounds but broken. Dead for hours. She placed it back on the sand for nature to do its burial.

She went on.

Above, an aircraft flew quickly, never noticing Mistress Liennie. It was the commercial sort headed for a city, hundreds of miles to the east.

She saw it, followed the vapor with her eyes, and then proceeded westerly.

She was not inclined, as some were, to see the end of tradition with every passing of a machine. The tradition of monking was destined to stay in Hobarian life.

The prophecy of doom was not part of her.

"The Svids are too prominent in our life," they would say.

"Why allow Krits freedom of our world? They do not reciprocate with openness."

She always just listened or would end the argument by saying, "Do you fear that our ways are so weak they cannot stand questioning?"

Mostly, she was silent.

By this time, they knew her, trusted her. She had reached twenty-six years (thirty-nine Terran).

She had been a Mistress of the Circle early in her life. She had understood at ten what others just barely touched on at twenty. But Master Larr had pronounced her competent despite her youth. That ended argument and quieted suspicion.

By twelve, she had a school. By fourteen, masters were calling her Mistress. By sixteen, even off-worlders had heard of her.

Invitations came from Svid, from Earth. She would not leave Hobar. They came to her. Some were captured by her ways, others disappointed.

She was the spiritual teacher of Hobar. No one denied it.

To add to her fame, the Krits despised her. Most persons despised the Krits. Her fame spread to the thirty-eight worlds.

On Hobar, nature was still experimenting.

Its order was far from perfect. The coming of man had compounded the imbalance.

There were ripples in the sand.

Liennie gauged the source, the extension. Under the sand was a root: the herbivore's prime food source, man's most dangerous enemy.

Liennie drew a dart from her pack and broke the tip.

The root was traveling toward her. If it touched her, it would be death. The root would drain every fluid from her. Her proteins would be useless to the root, but it needed her water.

She had walked too far into its circle. She would need all her skill.

She turned slowly, her eyes downcast. One of the ripples was approaching fast.

The bluish-green vine left the sand and swung.

Luck! A clear shot.

The dart was imbedded and the poison was fast. It broke the protein mold instantly. The vine dropped, the sand flew as the rest of the root, gasping for air, rose to the surface.

It was too late. The root was in rigor mortis, dead.

The root, an attempt by Hobar at plant life, was passing into the planet's prehistory. Earth grasses, Earth trees, were stronger. The dread enemy of man had been driven into the desert. The herbivore had followed it. A blessing and a tragedy all at once.

The herbivore could be tamed but not made capable of feeding on grass. They would die together.

Liennie went to the source of the root, a sort of spoke, and cut deeply with the slim weapon now turned knife.

The root held a medicine. The medicine was costly to synthesize. The yellow powder she extracted would bring comfort to thousands in its diluted form and a great deal of money for her school. It cured certain forms of schizophrenia or brought untold visions and paradises (illegal paradises) to those who could steal it.

Liennie was interested in the medicine.

Visions and paradises were for the unbalanced.

She carefully put the powder in a transparent pouch which she hung around her neck and dropped inside her blouse.

Then she continued, leaving the dead plant for the next storm to blow away.

The storm was worse the next night. Her cube was at an angle most of the night and only righted itself when the winds died down in the morning.

The winds, she guessed, had reached eighty to ninety miles per hour.

The little village where her school was located, she didn't doubt, had had to rely on fields the night before.

Eventually she reached the mountain where she planned on spending her two weeks of monking.

The landscape distressed her.

Man-made grass. A post designed to project a field. Habitation.

She could not recall a village being put up there.

Then she knew. A sign written in Old English.

No Trespassing. Property of Krit Government.

Of course.

A section of land had been freely given to the Krits for an embassy. The worst of luck.

Her monking sword was buried on what was considered, in effect, to be Krit itself.

To be seen on the property would cause a diplomatic incident. Liennie was a good citizen. She did not wish to cause her government any trouble.

Yet if she went to her government to help her recover her sword, the government would be forced to ask the Krits.

The Krits, who considered Hobar a den of pagans, would never comply. They would destroy the instrument.

As bad, or worse, the secret location would be given away. Tradition forbade it.

Liennie wasn't long in making a decision. Where honesty causes difficulties, dishonesty was in order.

She dug into her pack for the instrument to cancel any sentry beam. It was merely the cube control slightly adjusted. Every Hobarian knew the trick.

It wasn't that Hobarians were basically dishonest. Quite the contrary. It was just that they understood that law and reality were not always in harmony.

A few hundred yards and she was looking at the town the Krits had built to house their embassy.

Her monking sword might as well have been hidden on Krit itself. Directly above where she had buried it, many Hobarian years before, was the main temple. No heathen could get within a hundred yards of it.

Certainly not by day, she thought.

Hobarian nights were something else. Few Krits would be out, force field around the town or not.

She found a grove of trees and climbed one.

It had been damaged the night before. Field protection of wide areas was far from perfect. She had difficulty finding enough shrubbery to hide even her small body.

Three hours to sunset.

She sat in perfect silence.

She watched Krits go through the grove on one business or another. Their lack of awareness of their surroundings shocked her. Surely, any of the students from her school would have spotted her by now.

But she understood, with the help of a scholar's game called substitution. It had originated with the twentieth-century psychologists.

To deny one thing had the consequence of honoring the opposite.

Look at the Krits with their heavy garments—cumbersome and impractical. And the men with their heavy beards.

Denial of personality meant denial of sensitivity.

What did they do with their time?

They prayed to a universal deity, friends had told her, usually adding that that deity was a primitive explanation of a wider phenomenon, complicated by personal terror and embroidered with all sorts of sexual misunderstandings.

Another scholar's game. Simplification.

A useful game, they pointed out, when one has to make life-and-death judgments. With the Krits, who would justify any action through their god, life-and-death judgments were an easy choice.

And then her friends would go on to discuss the Krits' tribunals and their judgments of death.

The women came on the second hour of Liennie's vigil.

One, a young woman, with deep eyes and humbled demeanor, spotted her. Like all youth, she had yet to be disciplined into unbending patterns.

Her wondering mind was matched by her wondering eyes. She didn't scream as she saw Liennie, who had put a finger to her lips. She understood the signal.

If anything, the youngster was confused, torn by curiosity and terror. She had never seen a Hobarian before.

It was an older woman, who, seeing the young woman and following her gaze, screamed.

Liennie jumped down. Three men came running and then four more from another direction.

Not quite caught.

One reached for her. He was thrown. Another received a kick in the midsection. Another, a blow to the chin. Unconscious. Two were guided into colliding into each other.

The sixth produced a projectile weapon, ancient but effective. It was twisted from his wrist and he howled in pain.

The seventh didn't have a chance.

A minute amount of time saw four unconscious and the other three on the ground in pain.

That same minute amount of time produced twenty more. Some had projectile rifles and the good sense to stay about twenty feet away.

Liennie stretched her arms apart in surrender.

They had two of the women bind Liennie, hands and feet, and carry her to a building. There she was locked in an unwindowed room with an older woman, who untied her.

"You will spend the night here for purification," the older woman said in Old English.

Liennie's understanding of the tongue was imperfect at best. In any case, she would have kept silent.

"They call me Lan. It is not a true name. Women have no true names among us. We are imperfect creatures not deserving of a name in the eyes of God. It is a title of the senior widow. I am of the house of Lazarus," she finished with some pride.

Liennie continued her silence. She looked around the bare room. There was a stool with a basin. That was all.

"Remove your clothes. You must first be washed."

Liennie complied.

"What is that around your neck?" She pointed to the clear bag.

In a poor accent, Liennie said, "The powder of the root."

"I'll take it," the old woman said.

Liennie handed the fortune over. "Do not breathe it in, Lan. You are healthy. The medicine is not for you."

The old woman ignored the warning as if it hadn't been given and placed the pouch in a pocket. She washed Liennie carefully, thoroughly, in a ritualistic manner.

Liennie participated in the ritual almost as an inanimate object. Her idea of cleanliness was to step into a shower when she felt dirty and to let the processed waters do the work.

This was far different.

The woman produced a garment which covered Liennie from neck to toe. "When you step from the house, you must cover your head. Remember that!"

"What's to happen to me?"

"What happens to all women. When you die, you will see Limbo."

"In this universe, I mean."

"You have been saved from your sinful ways. We will pray."

The old woman knelt. Liennie followed suit.

They knelt for hours in silence.

"We will sleep now. I will show you how to decently lie down. Always lie on your left side, like this, putting your left hand under your head and your right over your side, above your waist. Sleep now!"

Liennie slept.

In the morning there was more silent prayer until a click in the lock was heard.

A bearded man walked in, followed by two guards with rifles. "Leave, Lan!"

The old woman left quickly.

"Can I order these guards out?" he asked Liennie in contemporary English.

"I won't harm you," she said.

He gestured and the guards left.

The man produced a document from his pocket. "You are Liennie?"

She bowed.

"What brought you to the village?"

"I was passing this route. I did not know it was the Krit Embassy."

"You hid?"

"I feared. When can I leave?"

"Never. You are a woman. You must have our protection. You are part of the community now. We forgive your past sins."

"Thank you for your kindness." She knew that she would have to escape.

"Your sincerity is in question. You will be guarded for the present time. You still have the devil's power about you."

"Master Larr taught me. He was no devil," Liennie objected uselessly.

The man left and locked the door behind him.

A few minutes later, the old woman returned to let her out.

"I am told to tell you that there is no way you can leave widow and virgin house. There are guards with instructions to dispatch you if you do."

"I'll cause you no trouble," Liennie assured her.

"You will work an hour. Then you will eat the morning meal."

Guarded by the old woman, Liennie was set to scrubbing a floor. She did an excellent job.

She was then escorted by the same old woman to the kitchen. "You seem to be a willing worker," Liennie was told. "You are a novice and yet older. Perhaps, I will assign you to weaving anyway." After a moment, the old woman added, "It is a desired skill."

"I will try to be worthy," Liennie said.

The kitchen was large enough to accommodate the thirteen, now fourteen, unattached women who were part of the clan assigned to embassy duty. It had no modern facilities that Liennie could recognize. . . . Everything seemed to be done by hand.

Liennie wasn't sure whether this was for religious purposes or simply because of the lack of status the Krit women apparently had.

"You will sit at the end with the unmarrieds," she was ordered.

They fed her some gruel. It was nourishing enough, Liennie decided, but quite tasteless.

The breakfast lacked formality, almost as if livestock were being fed.

After the meal, she was shown to a foot-operated loom.

Within an hour, she had mastered its intricacies. This surprised her teacher, the same young girl who had first spotted her. Within two hours, she was better than her teacher.

Within three hours, Liennie understood all the possibilities of the simple machine.

Her teacher panicked. Never had she seen anything like it. Only the devil could give a person such skill. She ran to Lan, who came rushing back.

Lan was cautious. "Have you ever operated a loom?"

"No," Liennie said. "I have operated other machines. I am accustomed to work."

"Continue," Lan said, apparently satisfied with this explanation. Then she left them.

Liennie understood her strategic error and held herself back. She had no desire to embarrass these women.

There was an unnatural silence among the women. If the stranger were not present, there would have been chatter. Liennie could sense the urge among them to say something. It was up to her to break the silence.

"On Hobar, we also make our own garments," she bid, "though we buy our material from manufacturing plants."

No one spoke.

She tried again. "Do you also stitch or is that left for other women?"

The young girl answered, "We stitch."

Then silence.

They were taken for an evening meal, which was eaten in silence.

Then more time on the looms.

Then prayer and bed.

The next morning, Liennie was left alone with the young girl. She guessed that the other five who had been in the room had additional duties.

The young girl had facile hands. She did the fine work on a full-time basis while the others apparently were recruited only once in a while for mass production of raw cloth.

Liennie was left there because she wasn't allowed out.

"What is your name?" Liennie asked.

"I am referred to as Du, the Illegitimate. I am tolerated. My parents faced the Tribunal. I was adopted out of kindness but I shall not see Limbo."

Liennie wasn't familiar with the intricacies of Krit theology, although the young girl was assuming that she was; but she didn't want to press her and so answered, "I am Liennie of Ib Village. I too have been adopted. We shall be friends."

"It is forbidden."

"Then we shall be secret friends. I think we have been since you first saw me in the tree."

The young girl was silent but eventually nodded in assent.

It was three more days until Liennie was summoned before the ambassador. To say the least, the ambassador considered himself more a missionary than a diplomat. He looked on Liennie with a cold gaze.

He dismissed the guards. "We shall speak frankly," he said. "You are Liennie, the Liennie of Ib School." It wasn't a question.

Liennie nodded anyway.

"In a way, you are a spiritual leader of your people. Tell me what you teach in your school. Be assured that I am not blind to Hobar's ways, sinful as they are.

"I am not blind," he repeated. "I am assuming of your ways, the best of motives. We in the hierarchy are well aware of spiritual history. I am a Chief Hierarch as well as leader of my clan. You may be frank with me."

"I teach the ancient wisdoms as best as my ability allows. My spiritual forebears go back two thousand years before we left Earth, back to the ancient land of China," Liennie answered.

"You teach violence," he said.

"I teach peace. The strong are peaceful. The weak rely on machines for their violence."

"You object to guns?"

"Guns are designed for one purpose. The human heart knows compassion. I injured none of your countrymen."

"That is true. I hold no quarrel with your defense of yourself. We must have seemed as enemies. You practiced charity."

"Then you will allow me to leave?"

"I would prefer you saw the light."

"I have respect for your beliefs."

". . . But you do not believe?"

"I do not believe," she agreed.

"We will teach you to believe. You will stay with us."

"No," Liennie said, "I will not. You cannot hold me in bondage and expect me to follow your ways. If you wish to try to convince me, you must allow me my freedom of movement."

"You are on Krit soil, Mistress Liennie. Here, your rules do not apply."

"The rules of my nation do not apply," she corrected. "My rules do."

The hierarch pressed a button and two armed guards appeared.

"Beat her," he ordered and left.

One guard trained his rifle on her and the other placed his weapon against a wall. He approached her and swung. Liennie avoided the blow by turning slightly. He swung again, and again she avoided the blow. She moved much faster than he did. She didn't raise her arms against him. She was like a shadow.

Finally, the guard gave up and walked away.

The other said, "Do not move or I will fire."

The guard returned with help. Two men took her arms while the other struck.

The man had no mercy. He showed no charity. He beat her into numbness.

They carried her back into the widow and virgin house.

Du was assigned to minister to her. "I am often beaten," she said to Liennie. "You will get used to it."

Liennie had no intention of getting used to it. Tonight she would escape. "Will you let me adopt you, Du?" she asked the girl. "I will never beat you. You will find a husband here on Hobar and forget your bastardness."

"It is a sin for me to marry."

Liennie had guessed that much. "I am the head of my clan. I will make you a full member. There will be no sin."

The girl applied the lotion to Liennie in silence.

She finally said, "Yes, I will go with you. How will we leave?"

"Leave that to me." She rose and went to the door.

It was locked but it was wood.

"You must have faith," Liennie said and struck the door with the heel of her foot. It buckled. She struck it again. It broke. She slipped out.

Du heard a subdued cry and saw Liennie drag in Lan.

"She will sleep," Du was told. "Silence and soft movements are called for."

They had no difficulty leaving the house. A guard would also spend a restful night.

"Stay with me, Du," Liennie said softly.

"The temple. No woman may approach the temple!" An agonized protest from Du.

Liennie realized that there was little point in arguing. "Go to the tree where you first saw me and climb it! Wait there! Be silent! Be careful!"

Du nodded and left.

Liennie went to the temple. She climbed a wall.

A guard on top didn't see her. His rifle made a minute but sharp sound as it fell from the roof.

Liennie entered through a second-story window.

It was an office. She searched. Nothing.

She searched another. Better luck. Her pack and clothes were there, intact.

She also found a receipt. Her powder had been sold.

That was a matter for the civil courts. Later.

As she entered the worship area, she judged that her monking sword was buried underneath the second pew.

She drew from her pack the weapon intended for the eight-ton mammals. She reset it. A small thin beam dislodged the pew. She dug with it, skillfully and with purpose.

She hoped the green beam wouldn't be seen.

It wasn't.

The sword was in her hand. She left the same way she came in.

To the grove. To the tree.

Du had seen her approaching. She had climbed down.

Silently they made their way to the village border.

The field was glowing red. There was a storm outside. From the intensity of the glow, it was a violent one.

They couldn't stay. Already, she saw lights behind them. They had been discovered.

"This will be painful, Du," she said and produced a cord. She tied it to Du's waist and her own.

"Have courage!" She put her only pair of sand goggles on Du's eyes and broke the field with her weapon.

Immediately sand was on them. It blinded but it also covered their flight.

Liennie felt the numbness of the intense cold come on her. She moved forward a hundred feet. She thought she heard Du cry but couldn't be sure.

When Liennie was sure they were past the border, she hurriedly struck her tent field.

Warmth.

Du, the Illegitimate, huddled close to her.

"It is almost over, child," Liennie said. "They cannot touch us. We are safe.

"The field will protect us. There is enough food. I prepared for a two-week monking."

Du slept holding on to Liennie. Liennie kept vigil.

Morning came but Liennie didn't break the screen. That would have been suicide. She made it clear as glass.

She had guessed correctly. Eight men surrounded her tent.

Behind them, she saw the border; a sand dune covered the place of their escape.

The voice was tinny but clear. "Come out or we fire."

Liennie checked her control. It was correctly set.

Bullets disappeared in a flash against the screen.

"We have a disrupter," the tinny voice said.

Liennie knew it was lying. By treaty, no such weapon was allowed an embassy.

An hour passed.

"We can wait longer than you can."

Liennie wished that she had a radio, but what use would a radio have been on a monking? She was counting on something else.

She watched the sky. The vapor trail came on the horizon. She bided her time.

The tents weren't made exclusively for monking, she knew. The clever Svids who made them included other features intended for explorers.

She made the field shine. It could be seen in any environ for ten thousand feet. In Hobar's relatively clear atmosphere, it could be seen twenty thousand feet.

The commercial aircraft flew at eighteen thousand.

If it didn't see her today, then tomorrow or the next day.

Two hours later, three police aircraft converged on the scene.

Hobarians, being naturally distrustful of Krits, especially in the area of their embassy, had come prepared for any contingency. They disarmed the assailants quickly.

Liennie broke the tent and told the police lieutenant, "This girl is under the protection of my school."

"She's ours," the Chief Hierarch insisted.

"The courts will decide," the lieutenant said and gave a sly wink to Liennie. The lieutenant was one of her students.

The Chief Hierarch looked sternly. "I condemn both of you to hellfire. I hope I never see you in this life again," he added to Liennie.

But Liennie knew that he would.

There was the matter of her property being stolen and sold.

Still, she kept her silence.

CHAPTER ONE

POLITICS

Peer Shear sat back in the limousine, occasionally glancing out of the one-way window. Earth was crowded, he thought, even more than Svid. Unlike Svid, Earth was crowded in an unorderly way, as if the past imposed on the present. Architecture was radically different from yard to yard, it seemed. Peer decided that this was all pleasant.

"You're looking out the window like a tourist," his companion said with amusement.

"I am," Shear admitted.

"I thought you made the Earth run now and then?"

"Yes, I do, though I rarely leave the outport. This is my first trip to the capital."

"Nice is very pleasant," the companion agreed. "Did you know that we're on the southern coast of old France? This place has some of the most pleasant weather in the inhabited worlds. People pay a king's ransom to vacation here."

"Can I afford it?" Shear asked jokingly.

"Yes, especially since the Confederation is paying. You are part of my delegation, you know."

"Only officially. You know I gave my word to Liennie."

"Do you think I want war?"

"Yes," Shear said.

"Well, it should be interesting to have Mistress Liennie oppose me. Do you think she can defeat me in my realm of politics?"

"She had the Council force me on your staff," Shear pointed out.

"Her influence is with the Hobarian Council. She is hardly known on Earth. You'd best not forget that sixty-two per cent of the Confederation population is on Earth. They have the votes in the House and I am Speaker."

"There's the Senate," Shear said, "and our three Senators are of Liennie's school."

"You certainly have a great deal to learn. The Senate is only a ceremonial body originally designed to pacify the unhappy thirty-seven worlds who could so easily be outvoted in the House. It has no real power."

Shear turned from the window and smiled. "It has the power to perform ceremonies. Ceremonies can be very important."

Shear's companion smiled. He was like a sheep among wolves. The companion doubted that mingling among the Confederation bigwigs would much affect Shear's ego, but he would be easily fooled by outright lies. Shear was an incredibly open and honest man who could understand thievery and cheating as long as it was underhanded, but an outright lie—that would be impossible for Captain Shear to comprehend.

Shear returned to the window.

The limousine passed a store that said on a large sign, "Find the Truth. Pray for Salvation. Understand the Nature of God. The Public Is Welcome." Each statement was neatly placed one under the other and easy to read.

"Are the Krits making inroads on Earth?" Shear asked.

"Sixteen million followers," the companion said. "They have nearly overwhelmed the remnants of the Old World religions. You can imagine the problem we face."

"How about the Circle?"

"The Circle suffers a disadvantage," the companion said. "It is based firmly on truth, which is hard to harness to political purpose. Other problems with it are that it takes so long to understand the rudiments and the rudiments can't be expressed clearly in language. Should I continue?"

"Yes," Shear said. He understood his companion to be a shrewd observer and wanted whatever opinions she offered. He had known Captain May Mahat for a long time. She had no intellectual weaknesses.

"People play a magic game with words. It compensates for their powerlessness in an indifferent universe. You cannot trick with the Circle. The worse instructor knows enough truth to command followers. He just can't hold on to them. Here on Earth, I've met six persons who might reasonably qualify as followers of the Circle and none of them are anywhere near your proficiency, dear Peer."

"I thought we had hundreds of instructors here," Peer said.

"We do but they are mostly incomplete masters. Most are charlatans. Why don't you visit one of the schools in the capital?"

Shear followed her advice. The next day, after getting lost finding the place in the old section of town, he arrived quietly and unannounced. He hoped his Earth clothes would sufficiently disguise him. Hobar was a sparsely populated place, barely a million inhabitants. A person like himself, who had taken part in the civil life of the planet, might easily be recognized.

He sat in the spectators' section, having been handed a brochure by an Earthling assistant to the instructor.

The instructor entered the gymnasium followed by his students. He turned to the dozen or so visitors and said, "Welcome. I hope that what you'll see will convince you that the Circle is a worthwhile pursuit. My assistant will direct you to my office if you care to join these classes. There will be no request for money. Your support is entirely voluntary. Contrary to popular notions, there is no magic to the Circle. It is simply a way of concentrating your energy so that you will be healthier and, hopefully, happier. A slight consideration of the Circle is that you will, with diligent application, become a good fighter. But you will discover that you will also become more peaceful. Life will run smoothly. You will be more agreeable to your family and friends.

"So that there is no misunderstanding, I am not a master of the Circle. On my native Hobar, I would be considered a bare beginner. But conditions being what they are, I am considered qualified to teach on Earth due to the scarcity of really qualified people here. Some of you will therefore have to go to Hobar to improve beyond my meager abilities. Proper licenses and letters from the Albert School on Hobar to attest to my qualifications are available in the office for your inspection. My students, at my insistence, call me either Instructor or by my first name, Robert. Please do the same.

"If you had hoped to find a leader to follow or a person to worship, the Krit Church is two blocks away. We have no connection with paganism."

At least he's honest, Shear thought.

The instructor proceeded to instruct his class, completely ignoring the gallery.

Shear watched with interest. The man was no mere beginner but he was no master either. He reflected the classical training the Albert School was famous for. Sheer had avoided the well-advertised schools and had deliberately picked this obscure school from a listing.

Two hours, and all but three of the spectators, including Shear, had left. By the time the class was over, only Shear and a young woman were left. The instructor walked up to them.

"There are usually no spectators left by this time," he said and turned to his assistant. "Lock the door."

Shear smiled. He sensed that the young woman would soon join the instructor's eight students.

"May I ask your name?" Robert asked the young woman.

"Doloris Sanski," she said.

"I would not ask on Hobar, but on Earth I must. Why do you want to know the Circle?"

She shrugged her shoulders.

"Do you have fantasies of having some secret powers over others? Is it your desire to have control over people?"

She didn't answer.

The instructor nodded. "Your eyes tell all. Your mouth can't open to lie and your eyes will not. I accept you as a student. Your attitude will change in time as did the attitudes of your fellow students. You're fortunate. Others run to the fantasies of the Krits."

The instructor turned to Shear. "I knew who you were, sir, from the moment you entered. I am flattered that the chief assistant to the Ib School should visit me. There are more famous schools in the capital."

"Only because they advertise," Shear said. "You do this planet a real service and honor Hobar. The others distract from the true purpose of the Circle with their promises of martial prowess."

"Will you honor my school by initiating our new student, Doloris?"

Shear nodded.

The instructor turned to his students and indicated that they form a circle while Shear led the young woman to the center. He faced her and took both her hands, four fingers on the underside of her hands and the thumbs on top.

"Relax," Shear said. "Look straight ahead. Close your eyes if you want to. Keep your mouth slightly closed with your tongue on the upper palate. Breathe slowly. Now try to feel every part of your body; be conscious of every part. Feel the air go down into your stomach, slowly. Breathe with me."

Then he was silent. Technically, this was "the moment of transformation." It was based on an ancient psychological truth. Two persons in touch with each other operated similarly on a biological level for that instant. The better the instructor was, the better the rapport. It gave the student a view of things to expect and made instruction much easier.

Shear let go at the proper moment.

"I'll see you next week," the instructor said to the young woman.

A few moments later, Peer and Robert entered the private office.

"What made you leave Hobar?" Peer asked.

"I was a poor student, always concerned with status. I thought I'd get it quickly here. I did, but somewhere along the line I saw a flaw in my attitude. I gave up the downtown school to those of my assistants who wanted it and opened this one. I hear it prospers still. You must have seen the ads."

"Probably," Peer said, "there were so many."

"Can I offer you some food?" Robert asked.

Shear spent a pleasant hour with Robert and then caught a ground-taxi back to his quarters. He thought he had gotten a fair picture of what was happening with the Circle on Earth.

The organizational weaknesses were obvious and it was equally obvious that no responsible master would compromise it . . . war or no war.

Any compromise would mean that the Circle would regress to the martial arts from which it originated. The Earth-run schools clearly showed this. Few attended Robert's school and yet available statistics showed that nearly eighteen thousand persons in the Nice area alone were attending Circle schools. One day on Earth had taught him the reality of the situation as described by Captain Mahat.

His personal radio buzzed. "Yes?"

"Peer, where are you?" the voice of Captain Mahat asked. "The reception at the embassy starts in 0:15."

"I'm a half mile away, May. Plenty of time."

"Well, get here a few minutes late. We want to push your importance."

"Okay, out." He told the driver to drive around the block a few times.

"Ambassador Rikter," introduced Captain Mahat, "this is our special envoy, Captain Peer Shear."

"Greatly honored, sir," the ambassador from Rainbow's End said. "How do you feel about the latest Krit outrage?"

"My staff is studying it thoroughly. Action will be forthcoming," Peer said diplomatically. Aside to Mahat, he asked, "What is the latest Krit outrage?"

"A two per cent surtax on goods coming into Rainbow for missionary activities. The ambassador has asked Hobar to come in the district to compete."

"Wouldn't that violate the Aler Commercial Treaty?"

"Yes, it's a difficult problem."

A quiet conference followed the reception at the Hobarian Embassy. It was one of those key meetings that somehow lead to the reshaping of men and societies. Nominally, it started as a gathering of friends.

Peer Shear was there as a guest of Captain Mahat. So was Altaire, the ambassador from Svid, the most populous planet after Earth and one of the most technologically developed.

Between Earth and Svid, 87 per cent of mankind was accounted for. The Earth ambassador to the Confederation was there, the honorable Claymore Chase. He was also one of Earth's ninety-four representatives, sat on the dozen most powerful committees in the House, and was chairman of the all-important Interstellar Committee.

Hobar's ambassador, Lan Frate, was there, but everyone knew that it was Peer Shear who counted for Hobarian popular opinion and Captain Mahat who was the trusted politician. Frate handled routine diplomatic matters. No one knew this better than Frate, who quietly relegated himself to the background.

"You know Altaire," Captain Mahat said to Peer.

"Yes," said Peer, "our distinguished attorney for the Pilot's Association." He shook hands with his old friend. "What made you switch from the honest job of representing our interests to the scoundrel's occupation of ambassador from Svid?"

"My wife," the Svid ambassador said, and he and Peer burst into laughter.

"Altaire and Peer are very old friends," Captain Mahat said, excusing this apparent breach of diplomatic manners. "Altaire once saved Peer's position as a pilot."

"Damn right he did," Peer said. "He's the best union lawyer in the galaxy."

Ambassador Chase smiled. "I'm glad to hear that. Maybe we can save the union of planets with his skills. The situation is rapidly deteriorating. I dislike admitting it, but this gathering will be the closest thing to a war council in six hundred years."

The rest sat down in silence.

The ambassador picked a piece of meat from his plate. "Which doesn't mean that we can't enjoy this excellent Hobarian food." He looked around. "Dig in!" He smiled. "I'm ninety-six and I learned a long time ago never to think on an empty stomach. It makes you suspicious and dogmatic. 'Beware that lean and hungry look,'" he quoted. "That's Shakespeare. Most political intrigues were developed during his all too brief life-span. He knew!"

"We can always count on Ambassador Chase's wide knowledge of such matters," May said and picked up a fruit from the plate.

The Earth ambassador allowed the gathering to drift into a silent meal. He had the situation well in hand. He knew that these people had their minds on peace, except for Captain Mahat, of course. He knew that war was inevitable. He had to convince all the people in the room so that he and Mahat, whom he had picked for the key position of Speaker, could choose the most opportune time.

Mostly, he had to convince Peer Shear. Speaking to him was speaking to Liennie. Liennie's word would rally Hobar. She was the principal spiritual leader of that planet, the Mistress of the Circle. Chase knew she had earned every honor given her. Her support would go further than the word of Mahat, whom the Hobarians saw merely as their representative for economic interests. Hobarians, if anything, were spiritual people.

They would be the bulk of the military leaders in the coming war.

Chase looked up from his plate. "What have you to drink, dear May?"

She rose and went to the bar. "Does the ambassador wish alcohol?"

"Not tonight. My mind must not be sullied. I'll take a page from the Circle and drink fruit juice . . . the nectar of the gods."

"A toast," said Altaire, rising, "to peace."

"I prefer to drink to justice," Chase said, also rising, "but . . . to peace, if possible."

Chase sat. "I can understand Altaire's wish for peace. Svid is a merchant society, a solid pillar in the stellar society. But frankly, a delay in preparations for war would be suicidal. It is better to prepare for war and waste all that preparation than to go into a war unprepared."

"Yes," Altaire agreed, "but that preparation itself may lead to war. The Krits do not think logically. They will go to war with only three per cent of the population. . . ."

"And a considerable sixth column," Mahat interrupted. "They have more followers on Earth than on their own planet. We must defend ourselves. What they are doing to Rainbow's End is only a taste of things to come."

"Perfectly true," Chase said. "And for all practical purposes, they dominate Mora's World. A sad state of affairs. They combine a militant ascetic religion with an incredible greed and self-righteousness. Their people starve materially but they have that blinding religion. They make the militant Christians and Moslems of the past positively kind by comparison. Will we stand by, like old China, and be divided and redivided until we are forced by necessity to adopt an all-encompassing dictatorship to drive them out? It is better to fight them now, while they are relatively weak and parasitic, technologically."

"Your analogy is far from perfect," Altaire said.

"I respect your objections," Chase countered, "but the analogy is closer than you realize. Don't be too philosophical. The political reality is that Krit has half the interstellar pilots and Hobar has the other half. These eighty-seven thousand persons pilot our commerce through the faster-than-light void because they are the only ones who can stand the psychological pressures. Hobar and Krit nationals are the only ones who can be pilots, for all practical purposes, and they could have a stranglehold on the civilized galaxy, if they chose! Hobarian pilots apparently restrain their greed. That's the way they are. Krits want to spread their poison and aren't bound by any ethics from using their favored positions as pilots. Let's face it, the rest of us are helpless in suspended animation when we go from world to world."

Altaire knew he couldn't counter that truth. His own planet was forced into enough indecent compromises with Krit simply to deliver goods to the other thirty-seven worlds.

Peer pondered for a few seconds in the ensuing silence. "What will these preparations consist of?"

"Arming our ships. The technology is there," Chase said. "Meteor shields can become energy weapons easily enough. It is sufficient to know that our dear friends on Svid can work out the details."

Altaire nodded. "I agree to preparations, but no more at this time."

"That's fair enough," Chase said. "Hobar must prepare itself spiritually. I will see that materials on the history of warfare are delivered to the Hobar Technical Institute. Hobar, despite claims to the contrary, knows that the Circle has a martial history going back to the ancient Far East. It will be easy for them to adapt themselves to being our generals. Will it be preparation for Hobar, Peer Shear? You speak for Liennie."

"I was urged to plead for peace," Peer said.

Chase nodded. "If that was an uncompromising position, Liennie would not have sent you. She is not as mystical as some think. She is as practical as the Circle is."

"I will urge preparation and, like Altaire, no more at this time."

A sigh of relief seemed to pass through the room.

The meeting broke up. Captain Mahat and Chase remained in the room.

"The first thing you must do, dear May, is to urge your people to violate the Aler Commercial Treaty and give relief to Rainbow's End. It is justice under the circumstances. Your people will agree. And," he said with a wink, "it will anger Krit."

She nodded. "I will privately assure Ambassador Rikter but will wait until Peer communicates with kindly Liennie."

"Excellent. Oh, do you have any more of this delicate meat?"

Peer Shear left the embassy contemplating the meeting. For the first time in his life, he was afraid. War had always meant needless death. Rainbow's End would suffer most, and as for Hobar, he had four daughters and a woman he loved. Would a fusion bomb destroy all he lived for?

He took an aerial cab, never noticing that the driver veered from the route to his hotel.

He stepped out of the cab. In the split second that he realized that he was not near his hotel, the cab took off with a burst of speed.

He was surrounded by eight men, all armed.

"Will you come quietly?" asked the apparent leader.

Shear nodded. Never fight an enemy when he is prepared. These men, Earthlings, had probably been hired by the Krits, apparently without knowledge of the importance of their captive. He would work that fact to his advantage. They had no doubt been warned that he knew self-defense but men who rely on guns are usually overconfident.

They walked around him as they led him down an alley. Their mistake was clear. They were all too close. Shear would have had a man twenty feet behind. The alley narrowed and Shear struck five fingers into the groin of the man on his right and three fingers into the throat of the man to his left.

Two down.

He moved and broke two ribs of the man behind and cracked the jaw of his partner.

Four down.

At that instant, the lead men became aware of the fight. One turned and fired but Shear had moved and the beam struck and removed the head of one of his would-be captors.

Five down.

Shear disarmed the man and threw him against a seventh, knocking both out.

The eighth didn't wait; he ran.

Definitely hirelings, Shear thought, and disappeared from the scene. He recognized the part of town he was in and moved toward Robert's school. It would serve as a haven in case there were more assailants.

He found a burning building with fire-fighting apparatus finishing the job of putting out the blaze. He ran to a man who was clearly in authority.

"I'm the Hobarian envoy. What happened?"

The fire chief, a tired man, said, "It was a bomb. Six killed including the owner."

"Who did it?"

"We're investigating," the man said.

"Will you see to it that my embassy gets a report?"

"That's the procedure, Mr. Ambassador."

"Thank you," Shear said and walked away, overhearing the fire chief mumble something like, "damn religious maniacs."

He saw the young woman he had initiated that afternoon in the crowd. There was a stern look on her face.

His muscles tightened. For the first time, he understood the nature of the enemy.

Interlude

Dear Liennie:

By the time you get this letter, the events I describe will be three weeks in the past. I dare not trust Keller transmission and am sending it via our Circle brother, Geoffrey Lant. In fact, he should be the one to hand it to you.

First, you must pay our respects for Robert Druery, late of Albert School. He was murdered by Krit assassins when his school in Nice, the capital, was destroyed by fire bomb. I think this should be a personal mission on your part.

I did not know him well but you may assure his school that he represented them well on Earth. I took it upon myself to see to his cremation and to inform his two surviving students that they will always be welcome at Ib. His personal effects were also sent via Brother Lant. He has no family that I could determine. A further check through our police may be in order.

My mission has been an abject failure. I was honestly convinced that war is inevitable by politicians here. I was duly suspicious of Captain Mahat since she has been advocating purging the galaxy of the Krits for over twenty standard years, but I could not ignore the reasoning of Ambassador Claymore Chase of Earth.

Altaire, our great friend from Svid, also agreed.

To finally convince me of the hostile intentions of the sometimes sweet-talking Krits, Robert Druery was murdered by a young woman whom I thought sincere when I met her that same afternoon. I actually initiated her into the Circle. Only fanaticism could have fooled both Robert Druery and myself. Neither of us could be accused of stupidity in the matter of choosing students. She undoubtedly was instructed by expert Krit fanatics.

Forgive me, Mistress Liennie, but I must advise you to ask the council to prepare for war.

The following must be done:

One: Change the curriculum at Hobar Technical Institute to include military sciences.

Two: Transform our Circle schools into personal combat schools. (At least for the present, add whatever courses are needed and admit the general public to those courses.)

Three: Prepare for the defense of Hobar. Svid and Earth, more knowledgeable in these matters, will assist secretly.

Four: Inform the council to abrogate the Aler Commercial Treaty to protect our friends at Rainbow's End.

Five: Inform our planetary neighbor, Lak, of possible war. No doubt, they will want to co-ordinate solar defense with us.

It is my sincere hope that these measures will prove unnecessary, but frankly, I doubt it.

Please pay my respects to my dearest Du and my daughters. I am off to Svid.

> *In brotherhood,*
> *[signed] Peer*

Earth, July 7th (local)

CHAPTER TWO

THE STAIN OF THE PAST

Josephus Arin kicked the control seat back into the floor. He would attain transition in the Hobarian manner. It was, after all, the Hobarians who had trained him.

He was one of six pilots from Lak. He was one of a handful of non-Krits and non-Hobarians who had managed to become a pilot. It had been through the careful coaching of the Hobar Technical Institute that he had that privilege.

Hobarians would not commit the selfishness of keeping that profession to themselves regardless of the expense and trouble of training other nationals. It had taken him eight years to complete the three-year course. His pride had been affected until Hobar showed him how to transcend pride.

Unlike most Hobarian pilots, he was not a master of the Circle. His instructors at the Albert School labeled him competent and authorized him to teach off Hobar or to assist on Hobar. He had never availed himself of that great privilege except to teach his wife and children. He had overcome pride and had made peace with the indifferent universe.

The dials went wild this time. Machinery often did in the vapor universe that allowed material to travel faster than light. This was why robots were unreliable and men were still needed to transport cargo and passengers.

He centered his spirit and made the ship one with him. He would manually eject himself into "his universe."

Something worse than vertigo almost overcame him but he

held "control" over the magnetic bottle that held the Ctz radical. His left hand gently pushed the ball the exact micro-inch down.

He was in "his universe."

All that remained was to check the ordinary engine and his cargo. This was done fairly quickly, an hour and a half, relative time. All was in order.

He set the computer for deceleration from half-light, normal to 87,000 kilometers an hour, relative. Twenty minutes later, relative (a week, standard-normal), he would find himself in orbit around Krit.

Time enough for lunch.

He checked the pod that held his passengers by instruments. It was in the orbit-proximate to the control sphere that statistically had proved safest over the centuries. All normal—the passengers all slept well in suspended animation.

He would check it again before attaining orbit. Mechanical failure would be his only concern now.

He had a light lunch while the computer slowed down a message from Krit (he was still living "slower" than normal time). The message contained routine landing instructions in the stilted Old English the Krits continued to use.

He sent back a routine reply in Old Hebrew just to irritate the Krits and waste some of their valuable computer time. Ancient languages were his hobby and Old Hebrew had been spoken on Lak in the early years of colonization. It was also his way of showing nationalism, his last sentimentality, as he liked to tell his friends.

Once orbit was established, he moved the pods to trail the control sphere and saw to the safe strap-down of the passenger pod on the shuttle. It was his responsibility to see it to ground safety.

At the outport, he checked the dials with the port physician and signed it over to him. He took his night bag and went into the customs building.

Josephus grinned at the customs official, who stared back sternly.

"Lak?" the official asked with distaste.

"Right," Josephus said.

"Unusual for a pilot to be of Lak origin," the official commented.

"There are only six of us and six from Rainbow's End, five from Kal and thirty-seven from Earth, and a scattered one or two here and there," Josephus said, knowing the information irritated Krits.

"Trained on Hobar," the official said with contempt.

"Over thirty years ago, sir," Josephus excused, "before your program got under way." Actually there was no Krit program except on paper. They had never accepted an off-world student. They would not share anything with "nonbelievers." For form, they had opened a program to satisfy the Confederation but, alas, they had never been able to find a qualified student.

It was common knowledge that an applicant fared better asking Hobar.

Josephus asked permission to stay on Krit for three days before his ship was scheduled to make the run back to Rainbow's End.

"Why would an outworlder want to stay on Krit? Why don't you return to your cargo ship like the rest?"

"I'm not a Krit. I have to have dirt under my feet whenever I can. I have no discipline to speak of." Josephus took advantage of the Krit's contempt for Lak. His vengeance every time he landed made it all worthwhile.

Josephus was a spy and a smuggler. Not for money. Never for money. The spying served his sentimentality, patriotism. He was an agent of Captain Mahat, who had always looked after Lak's interests at the capital. Lak had little power. Their planetary neighbor, Hobar, had an abundance of power. Captain Mahat had done much for Lak. Believing he represented Lak in this matter, Josephus was prepared to do much for Captain Mahat.

He had taken on this despised run, unprofitable as it was, because no Hobarian was welcomed on Krit and people on Krit tended to ignore his movements. Did he not come from an inferior people, lacking in talent and faith?

He took out a perfume bottle and slipped it to the official. "Make your wife smell nice."

"I'm too pure for frills. My wife is virtuous, not a whore."

"Perhaps for your many women." This was intended as an insincere compliment. Krits were allowed one wife and as many women as they could afford. Status was measured by the number of women they supported and the money a man could afford to legitimize his bastards.

"Perhaps. But what does the Lak want in return? Laks give nothing away."

"An unrestricted pass. There's business to be conducted."

"They'd put me in Hell, alive, if I allowed it. The city is all you get . . . for two bottles. As you say, I have many women."

"What does it say in the *Book* about stealing?" Josephus asked good-naturedly.

"The same as it says about smuggling."

"You are a brilliant theologian," Josephus said as he handed over the second bottle.

He had what he wanted. One always asked for more than one wanted. All Josephus desired was free movement in the city. The admirable quality about Krits, Josephus thought, was that they were all so consistently corrupt. Societies that talked about virtue so much generally were.

He was handed his night bag and his pass. When he opened the bag later, he would find a bank note missing. He wouldn't be surprised. An experienced smuggler insured that attention was diverted by interesting amounts of money.

Josephus reflected that this was the eighth time he had been dealt with by the same customs official and the man acted as if he had never seen him before. Josephus decided that this was simply a sign of contempt. No one could be that unconscious.

Josephus was wrong.

Stepping out into the street, Josephus decided for the twentieth time that the capital of Krit was the dirtiest city in the galaxy. It lacked even a sewer system. As rich as the Krits were, they had no sense of civic duty beyond building ornate temples.

Josephus entered the dingy hotel and registered. Unlike other worlds, there were no pilots residing there. Most, unless they were Krit nationals, stayed on their orbiting ship, unloaded,

loaded, and left. The less they saw of Krit, the more they liked it. Their only contact with the planet was the half hour it took to sign over their passengers.

The hotel specialized in accommodating minor church hierarchs who came to the capital, which was called Portal, to seek some favor, dispensation, or the like.

The hotel was indeed dingy but Josephus' usual contact was one of those minor hierarchs . . . a heretic by Krit thinking.

Josephus had no special liking for the black-clad man who entered his room an hour later. He traded important trade secrets for heretic literature. Whatever he thought of Krit, he couldn't bring himself to like a man who betrayed his country. But he dealt with him. The information he obtained was important to Captain Mahat.

"Worm of a Lak, you have something for me?"

"A completely revised *Book* by the Great Heretic." Josephus could see the man's fingers trembling with anticipation.

The Great Heretic, who bore the more humble name of Alanis, had been condemned to death by the Tribunal of Chief Hierarchs but escaped to Hobar with no little help from a Hobarian pilot named Peer Shear, who had done it as a joke.

Since then, no Hobarian pilot had been welcomed on Krit. They could not prevent one from coming without confronting the Confederation, but hints had been placed and Hobarians never went where they were not welcomed.

"Give it over."

"Certainly," Josephus said without hesitation. He separated the strap on his night bag, pulled out a wire, and held it up. "Funny that the man with the truth of God could condense it all onto one wire. I heard there were six million words in this new version. An inspiring effort."

The Krit grabbed it.

Josephus pulled out a little box. "With this I can erase the wire to within, I'd say, one-hundred-thousand-mile radius. I have another in my ship. I don't mind pressing the button before I leave unless I get certain information."

"I have the trade reports," the Krit said—half in contempt and half in fear.

"Very nice. But I want more this time. I heard that Krit is preparing for war. I want to find out about it. Where are the warships, the war materials?"

"I have no such information."

"Oh well," said Josephus, and began to squeeze the box.

"Wait!" the Krit shouted in terror.

"I'll wait," Josephus smiled.

"I could kill you."

"The wire would be erased automatically if the ship stays in orbit twenty minutes too long. Stop speculating. I thought this all out, I assure you."

"Hobar must not discover this."

"My concern is with the fate of Lak," Josephus said in a comforting manner. "You have my word."

Josephus found it curious that all of a sudden, his word counted for something, especially since it meant nothing for the first time.

The Krit agreed to show him the new plant the next day. He would bring Josephus a proper uniform of a guard officer and accompany him.

As the Krit was leaving, Josephus pointed out that without a Svid computer, he could never transcribe the wire in less than a month. Josephus wanted no tricks. He wanted the Krit to have no illusions. Krits were known for their illusions.

Take the heretic Alanis. From his illusions and visions he had almost upset the entire Krit hierarch. Of course, prophets did crazy things like that. Actually, Alanis had died several years before. Even the best Svid-run hospitals couldn't save him from the accumulations and ravishes of diseases from years of neglect. His death was kept secret. A quiet professor on Svid now wrote his heresies. No point in ending the disruptions of Krit society merely because the Great Heretic was dead.

A certain satisfaction interfered with Josephus' meditation that night. He didn't mind.

Oh, for a fast ground-car, Josephus thought, the next morning. He walked silently near the Krit, whose wife and daughter followed close behind.

"If anyone asks," the Krit said, "you're my cousin Tolen."

Josephus nodded.

Even the road wasn't paved. Josephus found it hard to believe. If anything, the coming war would free the Krits from this kind of life.

"Remember," Josephus said, "one slipup and I destroy the wire."

"The plans I gave you are accurate," the Krit said nervously.

"They'd better be."

At the plant, Josephus left the Krits outside and jumped a fence. He would use his officer's uniform only if he was discovered. He preferred to work in silence.

He approached the plant feeling that it might be a trap. It didn't look like heavy machinery could be accommodated there. The building was barely large enough to accommodate a pod. Still, there was the possibility that the Krit had been misinformed.

A guard approached and said something to Josephus that sounded like a request for a password. A quick knife was thrown to the guard's throat and the body was hidden. Josephus was no Circle master. He didn't dare chance a fight against a man armed with a projectile rifle.

Guards inside the parameter didn't bother him. They saluted smartly.

He apparently belonged. He was now sure that they weren't building warships, but the plant was heavily guarded. They were building something important.

Once inside, he understood.

Androids based on the life form found on Allorg. Allorg had been off limits to the Confederation. "The possibility of intelligent life developing there is the closest possibility ever discovered," a report, two centuries old, stated. "Man may someday have neighbors sharing the galaxy. We recommend that they be untroubled."

Every pilot knew of Allorg. It was off limits.

The Krits had gone there for their androids. Worse, they were experimenting with bioengineering techniques condemned since the War of the Economic Determinists, six centuries before.

Unwittingly, the Krit traitor had given him information much more important than the location of warship construction factories.

Josephus spent another hour taking photographs with a hidden camera. Experts would be able to verify his findings.

He would go back to his ship immediately.

He contained his anger and extorted 20,000 units in hard Confederation currency from the heretics on the grounds that he had found nothing. He knew that he would never return to Krit peacefully. It was time to make up for his years of lost profits.

It also gave him a gauge on the power of the heretics. It was considerable. They raised the money in one hour. He should have asked for twice the amount.

He caught the shuttle to his ship.

He was tempted to erase the wire anyway as he entered the safety of his ship but reasoned that the professor on Svid had written the long-awaited revision of the *Book* with disruption in mind and so he restrained himself.

He coupled the pods with the energy fields and left the system.

He didn't feel completely safe until he entered the vapor universe.

Interlude Two: A Lecture

The chief of the Hobar Technical Institute had been giving this introductory lecture for thirty years, changing only minor technical details. He surveyed the 197 students, lowered his eyes, and began.

"Gentle people, I am Rass, chief here. The staff members will introduce themselves when they come forth to discuss the expectations and requirements of this school.

"My purpose in this introduction is to clear up misconceptions about the school. First, let me say that this school is supported by both the Pilots' Association and the Transport Combines' group for only one reason—to train pilots for transition travel. It so happens that the peculiar aspects of the psychology needed for piloting requires us to train you in many 'life subjects' that are highly valued by all Hobarians. But if you come here for this training only, you are acting as moral thieves, stealing an education meant for someone else. We ask that persons who do not truly want to become pilots quietly withdraw from this school.

"Since you are, to some extent, our responsibility, we will be pleased to offer counseling for some other course of study. Where needed, we will offer loans at no interest. Experience has taught us that poverty is the usual motive for persons who have no intention of becoming pilots claiming our scholarships. If you withdraw within the next few days, no blame will be forthcoming. It is understood that improvement of one's 'life sense' is a worthwhile goal that allows a reasonable amount of bucking institutional rigidity."

He knew that later, four or five students would approach him.

"Now, for the rest of you there are certain things that must

be understood. Ninety-eight out of a hundred have no difficulty
with the technical aspects of the education. Yet only sixty per
cent of you will receive pilot captaincies. The reason, you all
know, is that only some character types can maintain their
sanity in the uncertainty of transition space. The rest of the
people must rely on the comfort of suspended animation. In
the course of your three years here we will be able to determine
which are which. This is the only school where failure is no dis-
honor.

"Your time will not have been wasted, should you not succeed.
There are very many desirable professions which our failures
may enter. Some of them pay even more than captaincies. Naturally, none of them hold the prestige, if prestige is still important to you when you graduate. There must be some rewards
for the responsibility involved in transporting hundreds of persons from one star to another and being entrusted with valuable
cargo.

"It is a loner's job for Hobarians. We have a sense of individual
worth and equality that prevents effective disciplining of crews.
And equals may not operate together in transition without
murderous consequences. Your readings, while here, will give
you all the various theories about that. But basically it is experience that has been the teacher in these matters.

"For you, the discipline must come from inside. Regardless of
what theories come forth each year about the nature of transition
space, experience has taught us that the elements of a good
pilot are self-discipline and the certain knowledge of what he
is supposed to do. How else could you deal with uncertainties?

"Transition space defies our best computers. There must be
a man at the helm—a person who can feel through his body
that a magnetic valve is not releasing enough of the Ctz radical,
even when his instruments tell him differently—a person who
is not afraid of or for himself. Fear brings desperation or cocki-
ness. Both are evils in this profession.

"To obtain this discipline, we do not teach a military regimen.
Though that works moderately well, it is too alien to our culture.
Nor do we insist that you accept any one theory of transition.
That results in lost ships. The belief in firm theories makes men

do things that go against their 'feel.' Instead we insist that you learn thoroughly the Circle. It is the ideal discipline of 'feel.' Since it does not lend itself to institutionalization, we have no department to teach it. Rather, we encourage you to go to any one of the numerous schools around the city. We advise you to try as many as you think necessary until you find one that has the right 'feel.' Then stick with that one for the duration of your studies here."

Rass knew that every one of the students had enough proficiency in the Circle to have an idea of what school to go to. But he also recognized that his authority would re-emphasize the Circle's importance. There is always the possibility that a school with a heavily emphasized intellectual routine can make a student forget his balanced priorities. His own master of the Circle had once said, "Too much thinking makes the balance of a person rise to the head."

He continued, "I don't want to keep you here much longer, so I will only mention a few things about the Ctz radical. You've heard it before in bits and pieces, but I want to summarize it again so it will never leave your memory.

"One: It is not the 'Wrathful Hand of God,' as the Krits believe, nor is it the *Chi* or center of the universe, as some of our countrymen would have you believe.

"Two: It is a concept which substitutes for a process, and not a real thing. We call it a radical because it defies explanation by any of the known systems of physics. That is the only reason.

"And three: We only know how to manipulate it imperfectly, and that, through an incomplete technology—very much as our ancestors crossed Earth's oceans with an incomplete understanding of hydrodynamics. Perhaps someday, the genius will be born to give us the mathematics involved in forming the system of physics needed to understand the Ctz radical completely and we can all be replaced by efficient computers.

"But for the present I advise you to assume nothing about it, no matter how tempting. All that is known is that manipulation of the Ctz radical allows us to travel faster than light. Nothing else!"

CHAPTER THREE

THE COMMISSIONINGS

Almost to his amazement, Stephen Lock, late of the British Isles, now a Krit collaborator, found the interior of the Temple luxurious beyond his dreams.

"The representative of God lives here," explained the chief security hierarch, himself dressed in red velvet gown and hat. "You are a most important official now. I have it on good authority that you may be the first off-worlder to enter the Council of Hierarchs. You may even sit on the Tribunal if God is so inclined. It is apparent that God has plans for you beyond our meager human knowledge."

They walked alone down an immense hallway littered with art treasures of the last seven centuries. It gave truth to the notion that strict discipline made for the greatest craftsmen. Krit was a nation of strict discipline.

"Of course, there is the universal Contrary. He may be tempting us with your talents. We must test you, Stephen."

The Englishman said, "I stand ready to serve. Surely my record shows loyalty to God through his human representatives."

"The Contrary will often be loyal until the critical moment. Here we are." The security officer opened a door and led Stephen to a courtyard.

There were at least fifty individuals strapped to wooden crosses.

Stephen smiled at the picture. "This is what is done with heretics?"

"Only the important ones, Stephen. It is a rather expensive

process. A disintegration chamber costs almost nothing to operate and is efficient and fast in wartime."

"Who is this one?" Stephen pointed to a large bearded man.

"Not only a heretic but a traitor. He was caught with a revision of the *Book* allegedly written by Alanis. Intelligence suspects that it was actually written by a Svid professor. Intelligence thinks Alanis has been dead for some years now."

"Was he able to tell you?"

"No. Under drugs, we discovered only that he believes Alanis wrote it." The security officer went on. "That heresy is pretty much under control. I was more concerned with the military information he supplied to our enemies. It was considerable. Our whole Allorg operation was exposed. Under drugs he revealed a great deal. The ignorant fool actually took a Lak pilot to the experimental station thinking it was a space vehicle assembly plant. We found an enlisted man with a Hobarian-style knife in his throat and a number of workers there reported seeing a strange officer lurking about on that day."

"How did you catch him?"

"Pure accident. He was a minor hierarch in a rural pastorate. Our random checks of his church books found he had sold a number of church items. Several thousand units could not be accounted for. He was routinely drugged and it came out."

"Now he will be killed?"

"Yes, after we allow him to languish there a few days. T[ ] morning he watched his wife and daughter die. A special integrator slowly removed their limbs, one by one. The [ ] niques are a high art. We can keep the subject alive for ho[ ] introducing certain drugs and monitoring the effect by ele[ ] After that, we dropped his infant child into a ditch, [ ] kerosene over it, and lit the fire."

"How did he react?" Stephen asked.

"He said, 'They die for the Truth,' and watche[ ] A fanatic. The Contrary does his work well. Alanis [ ] the most threatening heretics. If the Contrary canno[ ] to us with the Hobarians, he strives for internal disp[ ]

"God is strong," Stephen said.

"God is strong," agreed the security officer, "[ ]

the Contrary for whatever reason. We must also be strong. Hence we must test you."

"How will this test be done? I will endure whatever torture is necessary."

"A test of theology is really all that is required. A test of how well you've examined your own notions of what Krit is about."

They re-entered the hallway.

The security officer said, "You know that the prevalent notion of the universe has been that it was just. When that was proved unacceptable, since notions of justice proved to differ from place to place and from time to time, the prevailing notion became that the universe was indifferent. Hobarians still believe that. But that too is wishful thinking. If God wasn't concerned with justice, then he had to be indifferent. That was the rationale of fearful men.

"Actually, we know that God is interested in the universe but not in our notions of justice. He wants to be obeyed and that is all. He is unconcerned with us. He does not love or hate us. He just wants to be obeyed absolutely. The reasons are His. At this moment in history, He has chosen Krit to be His vehicle and the Chief Hierarch, His agent. He wants to destroy the Contrary's temporal powers. We will therefore make war on them and He has chosen you as His general."

"I am honored," Stephen said.

"Good. We know that the Contrary has misunderstandings about theology or he would bow to God. These misunderstandings are apparent in some subtle way in all his agents. So we will test you . . . with drugs."

"I am ever obedient."

Stephen was taken to a clinic and rolled up his sleeve. He went under and awoke several hours later.

"You are a Contrary agent," the security officer said, "but an unwilling one. You may still be saved by removing yourself from this universe."

Stephen's heart missed a beat. "What must I do?"

"Jump from the North Tower!"

Stephen got up from the table and walked out. He wasn't

followed. Without hesitation, he climbed to the North Tower and hurled himself to the cobblestones.

About four feet before striking bottom, his fall was stopped. He felt heat along his body. Suddenly, he fell the remaining four feet.

The security officer was waiting just inside a doorway. He smiled. "Drugs aren't perfect. This test is. You will find that your arms are slightly burned. A small price to pay to be in God's glory. Our force field isn't the best in the universe.

"I'll take you to the Chief Hierarch and then to the War Council."

The absolute Chief Hierarch was nothing like his picture. He was a large man certainly, but more fat than muscular. The blue velvet skullcap seemed to distract from his features. He was also the only Krit Stephen had ever seen close-shaved.

Stephen himself was shaved. A special dispensation because of his underground role. He had suggested that all the non-Krit faithful be allowed this dispensation in light of the fact that they might be identified. The suggestion had been rejected. It was too high a privilege to be widely distributed.

This would cost the Krits many potential fifth columnists in the coming war. It would cost them especially dear on Earth where they had the largest following.

The Chief Hierarch looked at Stephen. "I concern myself with tactics only in a general way. I confirm you General of God's Hordes. That's all." He went back to his reading of the *Book* and Stephen was led out to meet the Space Marshal and the Council.

The Space Marshal was a native of Krit. Nominally, he was under Stephen's direction but Stephen understood that this man would have to be convinced rather than ordered. Stephen had much political experience. He had been Deputy Chief Monitor attached to the Confederation Legislature for fifteen years prior to his treason. That office amounted to second in command of all Confederation police forces.

In order to serve God best, Stephen understood, a closed mouth and the ability to blend into the background was necessary. Others would collect honors; he would serve God.

The meeting lasted only a couple of hours. Actually, it had been entirely for the benefit of the Space Marshal, so that he might be briefed on the plans the new general had long ago worked out.

General Stephen went to bed early that night. He stayed awake late. His adversary, he was guessing, would be the Hobarian Peer Shear—not a man to be underestimated.

He would have to strike first and fast. Rainbow's End would be the logical first target and Stephen's fleet would be prepared in three days. With Rainbow's End under Krit control, they could quietly overthrow the puppet government of Mora's World and control the sector.

The only fly in the ointment was the operation on Allorg. It had been revealed too soon. He would have to use half his reserves to defend it. On second thought, he thought it wise to use three-quarters. Four fifths of the android force was still being prepared there.

In the Confederation's place, he would fusion-bomb the planet, but he knew they would never do it. They were politically committed to save it for the Allorgs.

What they would do, he was sure, would be to attempt to take over by ground infantry; it would never work.

In the last ten years, he had secretly prepared for this war. There would be few stones left unturned.

He took the woman supplied him in his arms but fell asleep.

At that moment, 4,687 light-years away, Josephus Arin sipped the fruit juice supplied him by one of Liennie's students. Liennie was still in meditation and Josephus insisted that she not be disturbed. He had been early anyway.

The student had left him in the common room of the Ib School thinking that he wished a little privacy after the hectic flight from Svid to Lak, and then, in an ordinary spacecraft, the 37 million miles to Hobar.

Josephus felt unusually calm. Throughout his life, he had been a minor personality in a large organization. Circumstances were forcing him from the background.

The calm was because he knew he could accomplish the task before him. Like so many others, he was the right man in the right place. Unlike many more others, he had never attempted to fit into any particular mold. He had admired and respected the Hobarians without ever trying to imitate them.

His loyalty, he decided once again, was to Lak, bleak Lak, dependent Lak . . . but Lak. It meant co-operation with Hobar and opposition to Krit.

Others had ridiculed Captain Mahat on the basis of her rather high-handed way of doing things. Her domination of any situation went against the grain of most of her countrymen. They avoided her while recognizing her talents. He, on the other hand, had recognized that she had the answer.

It sometimes bothered him that he, a basically peaceful man, had worked actively for this war. Now that it was at hand, he felt calm. Millions would surely die.

Would the galaxy be the better for it?

It was for other men, in other places, at other times, to decide this.

He had met Peer Shear in a hotel suite on Svid a bare two weeks ago for the first time.

"I'm Josephus Arin," he told a guard at the door. "Would you tell Captain Shear that Captain Mahat has a birthmark on her left buttocks?"

The man didn't even smile. He went inside and emerged a few seconds later. "Captain Shear will see you."

The suite was appointed for high government officials, which a man like Shear had apparently become.

A man with Shear said, as the Lak pilot entered, "What's this about a birthmark?"

"A code," Shear explained as he rose to meet his brother pilot.

"May the sun shine pleasantly on Hobar," the Lak said.

"And on Lak," the Hobarian responded.

It was a greeting common only to the two planets who shared that one sun, a situation unique to the Confederation.

The two men grabbed each other in relief, like two friends who had not seen each other in years.

"When Mahat told me about you," Shear said, "I hoped to meet you. This is Altaire, a very good friend."

Recognition came. "I knew of Altaire," Josephus said, "our past Association attorney. He drew up my contract."

"Yes, I remember," Altaire said. "A curious contract, Rainbow's End to Krit and back. Very unusual for a Lak. Now I understand. You were May's agent. I had often wondered how she was able to supply the Association with accurate information about them."

"What news, friend Josephus?" Peer asked.

"All bad, I'm afraid. The Krits are preparing for war. They have violated the ban concerning Allorg. They have mutated the unfortunate creatures into semi-intelligent androids. No doubt the androids will be their shock troops. What I found on Krit seemed to be an experimental station. Probably the mass manufacturing of androids is happening on Allorg itself. At least that's the opinion of Professor Lester, my contact on Rainbow's End. I stopped there and came here secretly. I took the liberty of warning the Association branch to keep non-Krit pilots from proceeding to Krit. The Association chief at Rainbow's End can be trusted."

"You did well," Altaire said. "There's nothing stopping us now from gearing up entirely for war. Josephus, I think you should proceed to Lak and Hobar and give word immediately. I don't trust Keller transmission for this news, even in code."

Altaire summoned one of the security people standing by and gave him the name of two pilots he trusted. Earth would be warned and by rotation the other worlds in the alliance.

The alliance had deliberately kept most of the smaller worlds out of the picture, hoping to spare them from the coming war. In any case, if the Svid-Hobar-Earth triangle fell, there would be nothing these worlds could do.

Josephus' recollections were interrupted by one of Liennie's students. "She comes." The student bowed.

Josephus rose to meet the spiritual leader of a world. He bowed slightly and put his right fist in his left hand, the ancient peace sign that preceded even the Circle.

Liennie returned the greeting and begged him to sit. She herself sat on the hard wood floor in the lotus position.

He sat directly across from her, a few feet from her in deference to her status.

"Sit closer, brother."

He moved up to just a few inches from her.

"You are our Circle brother from the respected Albert School. Word has come from them to call you master."

"I am unworthy," he found himself saying.

"Not unworthy," she answered. "Give me your hands."

She took them, four fingers touching the underside and the thumb above. "Close your eyes and breathe with me."

He obeyed her gentle command. His thoughts disturbed him. How often had he tried to explain away these rituals with cynical dismissals, but how often they had brought comfort.

He felt all the tension, all his defenses drain from him. He knew he trusted the kind Liennie.

"You are a lonely man," she said, letting go after a few moments. "Your life has been filled with purpose but little comfort. What god have you been serving?"

"Pride," he found himself saying, very much to his own surprise.

"You must dispense with that god. Your work from now on will require that you be without pride."

"What work?"

"You are to be charged with the defense of our solar system."

"Me?" Josephus said. "But I'm not from Hobar."

"You're from Lak, our celestial sister. You are a man of learning. The decision was made on that basis. The Hobarian Council chose you and Lak concurs. You must not question their wisdom. To question them would be prideful."

"And you agree?"

"I do not question their wisdom. They sent you here to see if you were a true brother. My role was to confirm their decision. I do so without qualm."

Josephus was speechless.

"Will you be my guest for a few days?"

"There is a great deal of preparation . . ."

"First, you must prepare yourself."

He bowed to her wisdom.

Liennie left him alone in the common room. He remained in the lotus position for many hours. Josephus, the self-centered, prideful man drained away, and Josephus, the general, emerged.

He found peace on the eve of war.

At that moment, 7,863 light-years away, on Svid, Altaire awakened Captain Shear. He handed the Hobarian a document.

Captain Shear broke the seal and read. "I am to be General of the Fleet. It lists my commanders, too. Arin for Hobar and Lak, Mahat for Earth, Chief Monitor Holt for ground infantry. You, Altaire, and Chase will be political officers."

"And for Svid?" Altaire asked.

"You are to name him."

"I'm not a military man," Altaire objected.

"None of us are" was the reply. "Who on your planet knows the most about Krit ways and the history of tactics? He does not have to be a pilot to command."

"Professor Jewette Lin" was Altaire's immediate answer.

"Then inform him."

Altaire nodded and left quietly.

Commander Shear sat on the floor in the lotus posture. His meditations went far into the night.

Professor Jewette Lin walked to the hallway where he kept the noisy *Transfax* transmitter.

One of his students had told him earlier that day that his friend, the Clown, had disrupted a state function again. The student had been excited in relating the details, the excitement stemming from an obvious admiration of the Clown.

Professor Lin had let him ramble on, resolving to get the facts from the conservative *Transfax*.

The professor dialed for the story he wanted from the newspaper, let the machine print it out, and went to his study to read it:

CLOWN IS RUDE TO HOBAR ENVOY ON ARRIVAL

Envoy laughs off incident as delightful. Says he admires institution of Clown.

Oberland Outport. Peer Shear, special envoy from Hobar and Captain in the Confederation Fleet, was mocked and abused early this afternoon by Arlin Elvuse, sometimes referred to as the Clown. Captain Shear's arrival with Svid special envoy Altaire this afternoon, notwithstanding the incident, was described by observers as proper . . .

Professor Lin was irritated by the *Transfax* article. As usual, the newspaper avoided the Clown's antics and reported only news of political significance. He debated within himself whether or not he should get a *News* transmitter as well. No, they would dwell on the Clown's antics to the exclusion of the context. There seemed to be no balance in the news media these days.

He would have to get the facts from Arlin himself, if the Clown showed up and if he was in the mood to talk and to answer questions.

"What seems to be troubling you, Jewette?" the unmistakable voice of Arlin said from behind.

Professor Lin turned. The Clown had entered from a window. This time, Arlin was dressed in a conservative business suit instead of the fool's costume he had adopted from Earth's Middle Ages. "Nothing except my curiosity about what you did to Envoy Shear. . . ."

"Why, nothing at all. The man is a master of the Circle. He might have killed me."

"You're not in the mood to be logical tonight, I see."

"What have you got to eat, friend Jewette?"

"Please answer my question."

"I'd like a beefsteak tonight, and if it's not putting you out, I think I'll sleep here tonight."

"If you promise not to bring any more strange women into this house again."

"Didn't I apologize? Oh well, I apologize now. Lovely girl, though." The Clown bowed humbly. "Admit, dear professor, that you like me around and I will answer your questions."

"I like you around," the professor admitted. "You provide an insight into this culture."

"Always the qualifiers," the Clown said. "When will you learn to live by your wits?"

"I have none," Lin said, exasperated.

The Clown chuckled. "You'll never convince me of that. A man who writes a piece of heresy—what was it?—six million words—for a religion in which he does not even believe—has wit . . . very great wit. Whatever made you spend so much time on the trite dogmas of the Krits?"

"An interest in human affairs."

"Nonsense . . . it was wit. I have a mind to throw you my mantle. You are the greatest Clown."

The house phone buzzed.

"That will be the police," the Clown said. "If you answer, you will have to lie. Leave it be."

"If I don't answer it, they will simply call me on my personal phone." The professor walked over to the phone, pressed the audio only.

"Dr. Lin, this is Chief Inspector Lavor. This time the Clown has gone too far. Tell Arlin to stay out of my sight for at least two weeks or I'll put an armed guard on him as surely as I hold my office."

"I'll tell him when I see him."

"He was seen going into your house, Doctor. I don't know why you protect him."

The officer broke the connection before Lin could reply.

"All you had to say," said the Clown, "was 'I'll tell him.' You talk too much. It will get you into difficulties."

"Please be silent."

"Then you don't want to hear about this afternoon?"

"Yes, I want to hear about this afternoon."

"Let's eat first."

Professor Lin let Arlin dial for the meals and watched the man gorge himself and go for seconds. All expensive imported beefsteak.

They retired once more to the study over brandy.

"What purpose is there in annoying an outworlder?" the professor asked.

"It wasn't for his benefit but for ours. This man wants war and Svid will follow unprepared."

"So you have a social conscience."

The Clown laughed. "I want to live in the style to which I am accustomed. What are the first things to go in wartime?"

The professor shrugged his shoulders.

"Why, the enemies at home. What better excuse than war to get rid of local irritations?"

"You're not an enemy. You're necessary to our sound health. You point out our pride and puncture it."

"A most logical argument for the scholarly journals. The intellectuals will make a feeble attempt to protect me. But they aren't the ones who man the guns. Anyway, I want to insure that Svid knows what it is buying. There hasn't been a full-scale war in six hundred years. A horrible hag to those who know war, it is a beautiful exciting virgin to the innocent. I spent yesterday looking at films of war. I read the propaganda. I sensed the hate needed. The Hobarians are above that. They are minor gods to be sure. But what of us mortals?"

"You think you can prevent war?"

"No," the Clown said softly.

"What happened this afternoon?"

The Clown took a sip of brandy. "I went to the outport to meet the shuttle. Peer Shear and Altaire were being met by officials. Polite words were being exchanged. So I screamed. My voice shattered the illusion that all was well. Then I went into a mock Circle ritual. As I expected, the officials turned red. . . ."

"And Shear?"

"The son of a bitch smiled. I approached him and punched him in the chest as hard as I could. He didn't even blink."

"And?"

"And nothing. The police converged on me so I left. As a Clown, I've failed miserably. I'm thinking of giving up the calling and getting an honest job as a gunner."

Altaire polarized the windows of the silent limousine as it made its way to Professor Lin's house. He was mindful of security.

The more he thought about it, the more the idea of Lin as commander of Svid defense made sense. The man had made a thorough study of history. He knew all the Confederation's cultures better than anyone living. He had been able to compile a heretic *Book* to keep the Krits off balance. Professor Lin commanded respect. Even the Clown, that irreverent Clown, never thought of crossing him.

He wondered why the Clown never bothered the professor. Well, it was understandable. The Clown had been his brilliant student at the university. No, that wouldn't stop the Clown. After all, he had had other teachers. It wouldn't be the professor's defense of the Clown in journals, either. The Clown rejected rationalizations. He accused Svid of being overburdened with them.

Altaire guessed what it was as the limousine pulled to a stop.

The Clown needed intellectual company, or, more accurately, a sounding board, a critic for his antics. He had to have a man of sound vision to relate to. Despite the insanity ascribed to him by the popular press, the Clown was far too sane for this temporal existence.

This made Altaire more comfortable with his choice for commander. He had trouble picturing the quiet professor in some sort of uniform at the helm of a ship.

Professor Lin answered the door and invited Altaire into the study.

Altaire saw Arlin sipping a brandy. "Might I have privacy with Dr. Lin?"

"Certainly not," Arlin said. "Not for the world will I miss the interchange between Svid's most prominent scholar and Svid's most prominent justifier."

"Look, this is national business," Altaire said.

"Can I get you a brandy?" Arlin asked with a smile.

"Professor. Please. This is a security matter."

"I won't breathe a word," the Clown said. "Don't worry."

"He can be trusted," the professor said.

"Yes, indeed, I can be trusted. Haven't you read the professor's learned article on the institution of the Clown? Deep honesty and a cutting integrity are essential to my business. None of my predecessors have ever broken their word. Why, Jock promised to retire to the university and did just that." Arlin smiled.

"The trouble is," Altaire said, "that this honesty may be a generational joke with someone along the way eventually breaking a confidence. Arlin may be the one."

"I don't think so," the professor said. "It would destroy the institution."

"It would indeed," the Clown agreed. "What a joke! Clowns, especially myself, have been getting too comfortable with the government lately."

"Like this afternoon," Altaire commented acidly.

"Only doing what was expected of me. Hobarians are far too noble to be left alone. Do you want a brandy?"

"Yes," Altaire said finally. "I guess I'll have to tolerate your annoying presence."

"Yes, you will." He handed Altaire a glass. "The truth finally comes out. It's not security but my offending nature. I'm flattered."

Altaire told Professor Lin, "I'm offering you the commission of Commander of Svid Defense. Do you accept?"

Lin was silent for a moment and said, "Yes."

"Not totally unexpected, I take it," said the Clown.

"I expected to be approached for a role in the war," Lin said, "but not as Commander. I thought the Chief of Police would be the logical choice."

"He will be a line commander," Altaire said.

"That's logical," said the Clown.

"I'm glad I have your approval," Altaire mumbled.

"We'll need a plan," Professor Lin said.

"I'll bet there's one in the safe," Arlin said.

Professor Lin walked over to his wall safe silently and extracted a sheaf of papers. "It will need some modifications, of course."

Altaire was flabbergasted. The Clown howled in laughter.

"There's no question about it," Arlin said, "I'm the wrong man to be Svid's Clown. Promise me, Jewette, to take over from me when the war is over."

"I might," said Lin, "just to silence you."

"Good. Look, Altaire, there's no need for a Clown during war, so I resign. I'll notify the government tomorrow. Of course, now I have no livelihood. You'll have to give me a commission."

"Is he serious, Professor?" Altaire asked.

"I think so."

Altaire thought it over. He wasn't going to waste talent. "Very well, report to the propaganda office tomorrow. You're a major."

"Where's the propaganda office?" Arlin asked.

"Wherever you happen to be," Altaire said.

"It took a war to bring out everyone's sense of humor," Arlin said thoughtfully. "I'll organize one immediately. We mortals must laugh on our way to hell."

Interlude Three: A Commentary in
The SVID TRANSFAX
(for interstellar edition)

The editorial "we" seems insufficient for this commentary. Let me identify myself. Gerald Bron is my name. This commentary is written with research by our staff.

Two days ago, Arlin Elvuse insulted the Hobarian envoy who has since become Supreme Commander of the Triangle force which, and let there be no mistake about it, will wage war on the Krits.

Elvuse has since resigned and was reported to be organizing a propaganda office for that same Triangle force.

The significance of this event may be lost on some of my off-Svid readers. Arlin Elvuse is probably a name they only know in passing and very probably do not understand the critical role he and his predecessors have played as Svid's Clowns.

The role of a Svid Clown is as old as the settlement itself and means a great deal more than a buffoon or a stage comedian. The Clown has always been the measure of this society.

The dim origins of Svid, made dimmer by the destruction of records during the War of the Economic Determinists, seem to indicate that the original settlers were a pious people, committed to commerce and community. According to what has degenerated to a legend or parable, they were so pious that they became forgetful of morality and became bound in ritual.

A deformed person dubbed Gerami was excluded from all rituals since he did not really fit. He was allowed to roam freely, eat where he might, sleep where chance left him, and abuse the citizenry.

He began to publicly accuse citizens of violating the all-important piety and was understandably put to death. Thus the institution of the Clown was born.

Svid still sees itself as pious to commerce and community and we have always had our Clowns, some better than others. Occasionally we have had more than one at a time; sometimes we have gone for a generation without one. In recent years, the Clown has even drawn a government pension whenever he chose to report an address. Elvuse was one of perhaps three of the most remarkable Clowns in Svid's history. At once a brilliant student of Svid culture and able to captivate the sensibilities of its citizens, his abuses were deeply felt and he was feared by both powerful windbags and small pretenders alike. He early recognized that poking fun at the personal habits of individuals only brought laughter, but poking fun at acceptable but shady practices brought enemies.

Elvuse was a successful Clown. He has many enemies, most of whom would use any excuse to hurt him though they keep silent because of the Clown's power and respect.

So Elvuse resigned, barely two days ago, after insulting the Hobarian envoy.

My conclusion: Elvuse knows war is coming. He feels threatened by his enemies who will certainly use the historical intolerance of war to get to him. His insult to the Hobarian envoy was designed to let Svid know that their fate is bound up with a planet which, unlike Svid, is without materialism, without what Svid understands as community. It was his last act as a Clown. There is no room for Clowns in war. Comedians perhaps, but not Clowns.

Elvuse is the first casualty of the coming war. He can never re-emerge in his former role . . . and he was a remarkable Clown.

Interlude Three (B): A Story From
The SVID NEWS
(Oberland city edition only,
later picked up by GKT)

Oberland North Suburbs—Professor Jewette "Doc" Lin today
told the *News* that war with the Krits was unavoidable.

He made the statement at a press reception where it was
announced by military spokesmen that the "Doc" was now Commander of Svid Defenses. He said that the attitudes of Krit
and Svid had never been reconcilable, but until the discovery of a
faster vapor universe, the tremendous distance between the two
planets had prevented a serious outbreak.

"It used to take eighteen months to travel between Krit and
Svid, sixteen between Krit and Hobar, and a full twenty-two
to Earth. However, since seven years ago, the average travel
time has been reduced to two to three weeks. The cultural
impact has been tremendous. There were 2,700 pilots ten years
ago. Now, with the reduced requirements, there are 87,000,"
the new commander said.

"Yet pilots still have to be mostly Krits and Hobarians. The
situation became intolerable. The Krits were pressing impossible
demands on Confederation members and the Confederation
couldn't stand for it. More than that, it is known that the Krits
are preparing actively for war. It remains for a first blow to be
struck."

The commander would not elaborate on who would strike it.

Asked if May "Mad" Mahat was behind the whole thing (it
is well known that Mahat has been war-mongering for the last
twenty-five years), "Doc" said that her feelings in the matter had

little to do with the real situation which was largely the doing of the Krits. Her role in the matter is that of a military commander and not a policy-maker; Altaire and Representative Chase are the political officers in the matter, he explained.

He was asked if Liennie of Hobar had been arrested, in view of her desire for peace. The commander said that her role was misunderstood. In fact, Liennie was the spiritual leader of Hobar. Hobar would never have joined the alliance without her approval and she would not have given her approval lightly.

She had to be completely convinced, Commander Lin concluded.

- 30 -

CHAPTER FOUR

THE FIGHT FOR RAINBOW'S END

Professor Kel Lester was awakened by his personal phone. He reached over. "Yes?"

"Kel, this is Mike. It's started. Better get over here right now."

"On my way." Lester jumped out of his bed and into a suit, telling his wife, "Prepare."

She also jumped out of bed and went to her assigned duty. In less than an hour, she would have the three communities on Rainbow's End evacuated of noncombatants.

In the small fast aircraft, Lester got on the radio, keeping one hand on the controls. "All right, give me the situation."

"Two fleets emerged from Vapor 409. One's twelve standard hours away. The larger fleet is a week away."

"How the hell did they get past early warning?"

"Listen, Kel, the small fleet emerged at the fifth line."

"Can it do it that close to the sun?"

"It did it and lost two ships as far as we could tell. They're not delivering cargo. They're taking chances. We figure the small fleet is the attack fleet and the other, the occupation fleet. They plan on staying."

"I see. I think Operation Scatter."

"Yep. That's what we figure. It's go for Operation Scatter. Unanimous vote."

"Get on Keller transmission and warn the Confederation. No need to keep a lid on this anymore."

"Way ahead of you. Already broadcasting. Wide beam."

Lester made his way into his cave headquarters and addressed his two co-commanders. "I say no heroics. Hit and run. There's only forty thousand of us. Keep them occupied until our fleet relieves us."

The two men nodded. One said, "They're going to be busy defending Earth and Svid. I think we're going to have a long wait."

"Maybe," Lester said.

An enlisted man entered the cave with a message.

"Our mines have destroyed six ships of the occupying fleet so far. The others have slowed."

"Maybe the orbital mines will decimate the attack fleet," someone said.

"Don't count on it," Lester said.

One of the co-commanders took Lester aside.

"Look," said the man, "when we blow the cities, where will we supply ourselves? This isn't exactly Earth."

"We'll supply ourselves off the Krits."

"I'm not sure," said the man, walking away.

Lester nodded in agreement. He had his orders from Shear. Hold and tie down. Three Hobarian super-cargoes had come for the children three days ago. They went into the slow Vapor 56. Eighteen months later, the ships would re-emerge. Lester was going to insure that those kids wouldn't grow up under Krit's savagery.

The advantage to small populations, Lester thought bitterly. What of the kids on Earth, Svid, Hobar, and the other thirty plus? Rainbow's End would suffer the brunt but her children would sleep safely in the hands of three very senior and experienced Hobarian pilots who could survive the psychic pressure of eighteen months in the vapor universe.

He knew that every man and woman on the planet would fight the Krits with their all. His wife had charge of the infirm and old. A mixed company of miners with the tools of their trade turned weapons was under her command. Not the best of troops, but all that could be spared.

The technicians and the skilled would give the Krits a taste of their own hell.

"Latest bulletin," a sergeant said.

Lester took the paper from the sergeant and read it. Attack fleet, twenty-seven controls and seventy large pods each. Orbital shuttles reported in pod orbit around controls. That meant 30,-000 troops. Occupying fleet, fifty-six controls with a variety of pods. Probably another 45,000 troops and heavy equipment.

Lester handed the paper to his two co-commanders. "I'm glad the Hobarian Liennie insisted that the children be removed."

"How long can we hold out?" asked the other co-commander.

"Until we're all dead. It's time for the two of you to go to your respective commands."

They saluted each other in the peculiar way inexperienced officers at the start of every major war in history had. They didn't expect to see each other alive again.

An hour later, the sergeant walked in again. "The Hobar pilot is here to see you."

"Send him in."

The man came in. He was still dressed in the coveralls of his profession.

"Didn't you get away?" Lester asked stupidly.

"Didn't expect the attack fleet coming from where they did," the pilot said. "It was either run or see to it that the bombs were properly placed in orbit. Also had to see that the heat-seekers at the eleventh line worked. "They do; scored eight total."

"Good! Thank you for staying."

"What do I do now?" the pilot asked. "I don't know very much about ground combat."

Lester smiled. "I'm an agricultural biologist trying to make this planet self-sufficient. You know as much as I do."

"You make your point well, Dr. Lester. I suppose I could train some of your people in hand-to-hand combat."

"That would be helpful. Sergeant, give this man some captain's pips. What's your name, anyway?"

"John Hodges, Doctor."

"John Hodges, it's good to have you planetside. Please make yourself available at 0300. I'll want you to have a look at those Allorgs. Maybe we can find their weaknesses. I have reports that they're nine feet tall and weigh in the neighborhood of 650 pounds."

Commander Lester, Captain Hodges, and two enlisted men watched from one of the rocky hills as the first Krit shuttle landed beside the abandoned capital. They saw the first squad of Allorgs come out of the ship. They were definitely nine feet tall and very probably weighed more than 650 pounds.

Lester handed the captain the field glasses.

The Hobarian looked at one of the androids. "Built for power, not for speed. I could defeat one in hand-to-hand."

"And my soldiers? None of them are trained in the Circle."

"A man of ordinary strength might be a match by virtue of endurance," Hodges said. "They're not built very well."

"My thoughts exactly. They've had only about ten years to design those damn things. I'd estimate that they're not very bright. No survival sense without an officer to order them about. Same problem the Economic Determinists ran into using androids. In the long run, men served better."

"Doctor, see what that Krit's doing." He handed back the field glasses.

"Yes, what a break! Remote control, not independence at all as we thought. Maybe we can jam the signal."

"Not likely, Doctor," the Hobarian said. "They're using lateral waves. The controls are probably palm-printed to each officer. Sergeant, see if you can pick off that officer."

"Yes, sir." The bulky sergeant took aim with the projectile rifle and removed the head of the Krit. The Allorgs immediately stopped their movements.

The Hobarian smiled. "Now they'll have to reprogram that squad."

A buzz bomb exploded the nearby hill. It had been launched from the shuttle.

"Time for us to leave," said Lester.

They kept low and eventually returned to headquarters.

"Bad news," Lester's adjutant said. "They're not entering the city. They must have been tipped off."

"I thought we had rounded up the church members?"

"They must have been wise enough to have a few shave," the

adjutant pointed out. "Besides, Major Kregg surrendered without a fight. A few of his boys got away when they got wind of what he was doing."

"They probably know our locations then. Give the word to open the secret orders. We're decentralizing as of now. Did you send that Keller out on the Allorgs?"

"Yes, sir, as soon as you walked in."

"Well, blow the cities. At least, they'll have to build their own quarters."

Captain Hodges said, "They'll find the Keller transmitter soon. Better blow that, too, or they'll confuse the Triangle force with your wave curve."

"It's in the capital. We've just been relaying by remote. It goes with the capital."

A rumble from distant explosions shook the cave. The room fell silent.

Finally, Lester said, "We built that lovingly. It was our passport to full status in the confederation. Do you think the Confederation will help us rebuild a capital as lovely as that, Hodges?"

"Better to build your own again, sir . . . whatever was promised."

Lester only nodded.

Lester watched Captain Hodges train his men. In the two weeks since the landing, they had little else to do. They had moved into the interior, but aside from a few rock-bound hills, there was little cover. Their attacks had been at night and limited.

It was becoming apparent that the Krits were there to stay for the duration. They had poured troops all over the countryside trying to ferret out the resisters. Reports had come that a good percentage of Lester's forces had been captured or killed. Many had been betrayed.

That fact bothered Lester very much. And to think he had voted against the establishment of the secret contingency orders. A good thing his two co-commanders had had more sense than he. Well, he thought, engineers always had more sense than biologists. He wondered how they were doing or where they were at this moment.

He had no way of knowing that part of his objection to the secret contingency orders had shown itself valid in the major defeat of his co-commander to the east. The man had not been able to call for reinforcements, not knowing where to call. A pinpoint radio was impossible to trace but useless unless one knew where to point.

The only meaningful hour, Lester thought, was when Hodges and his squad had brought that Allorg in for dissection. But what use was that information without the means to relay it to the Confederation?

"Very good, Sergeant," Hodges was saying. "Now try to keep your back straight. Not stiff, straight. That's it." Hodges withdrew to watch the husky sergeant shatter the rock with a gloved hand. "You see, gentlefolks, speed will give you strength. Relaxation is the best element of speed. The sergeant can now efficiently kill an Allorg."

The gathering clapped. A lieutenant stood up and said, "The sergeant has worked with his muscles all his life. I've sat at a console all mine."

"But you're a woman, Lieutenant. You have the advantage over the sergeant. He always took his body for granted. You're lighter. You had to learn. How else could you have brushed off all those unwelcome advances?"

There was general laughter when the sergeant said, "She's never had an unwelcome advance."

The lieutentant ran into the middle of the training circle and threw the sergeant over her back. More laughter. "I studied the Circle with experts for two years," she said. Still more laughter.

"I'm glad to hear that, Lieutenant. You're next to break the rock. Corporal, find a good fifty-pounder for the lieutenant."

The man trotted off.

"Now," said Captain Hodges, "comes the proof of the pudding. You can throw a man. Let's see if you can concentrate your energy. Put the glove on. It'll protect you from nicks."

The corporal returned with the rock.

"Hold it steady, Corporal." Hodges adjusted the lieutenant's posture, got her breathing right, and much to her surprise, she shattered it.

"Another Allorg killer," the sergeant shouted and picked her up.

"Put me down, damn it." She proceeded to box his ears until he did.

"How about the commander?" the corporal asked.

Lester shook his head no.

"Yes," said the captain. "You've trained as hard as the rest of us."

"Yes, yes," shouted the troops.

Lester, after some coaching, dutifully shattered the rock.

"Now," said the captain, "don't go shattering rocks on your own. I chose these for their porousness. They're about as strong as three or four Allorgs but some rocks are ten to twenty times as strong. We'll break up for the day."

Later that night, the adjutant and Captain Hodges were summoned to the command cave.

"Bad news, gentlemen. Orit has fallen on the east and Loist is barely holding on the west. It's a pincer movement. They'll get to us within two days. I've ordered the bulk of the people to move to the southern hemisphere and hide. I can't allow this planet's civilization to collapse. We've done the best we can. I figure that with two thousand troops, we can tie them down at least another week. If the Confederation isn't ready by then, there's little we can do. . . . At least fifteen thousand will escape. Any comments?"

"We're fairly concentrated, sir," said the adjutant. "They might use a fusion bomb."

"They can't and they know it. It would split this planet in two. The mass is wrong for that. That's why we've been so lucky at mining. Minerals which should exist a thousand miles down, exist two miles into the crust. It's a fluke that's working to our advantage. They want Rainbow's End whole. Our planet and Mora's World form a wedge with Allorg to protect Krit from a nearby staging area. Once captured, Rainbow's End will be easy for them to defend and supply."

"Then we need battle orders," Captain Hodges concluded.

"I'm calling the staff together in an hour for that," Lester said. He told the adjutant to get the staff together by pinpoint radio. After the man left, he said to Hodges, "You know, two weeks of war and we don't even have a battle flag. I've heard that Hobarians have a steady hand. Draw up one for me, will you?"

The pilot nodded.

"Oh, as much as I hate losing you, I could use a good colonel on the west flank. You don't mind?"

"No, I'm flattered."

The battle standard Hodges drew up was a red cat on a field of blue. He explained that the Krit Contrary was often portrayed as a red cat and his domain was thought to be the sea (at least to the theological illiterates).

It was widely distributed with the staff's blessing.

Almost at the predicted hour, Colonel Hodges' west flank was attacked by 22,000 Allorgs with heavy equipment and a Krit control section.

At that point, Colonel Hodges forgot about the two other fronts where, according to reports, similar difficulties were occurring. He concentrated on defending the ridge his battalion was holding.

"They'll walk over us," an officer said.

"Let's delay that as long as we can," said Hodges.

Land mines, rapidly constructed from mining explosives, quickly evaporated a few thousand Allorgs.

They kept coming.

The guided batteries quickly put an end to any attempt at air war. The batteries had been remotely-guided diggers and had been efficiently adapted to melt aircraft. Apparently, it took Krits to fly them and they weren't as self-sacrificing as Allorgs.

Hodges was happy to see the whole thing a ground war. He had the high ground and he would hold on fairly long. An estimated three more days were needed to insure the safety of the fleeing 15,000. In the southern hemisphere, larger if more unfriendly than the north, it would take years to dig them all out, and hopefully, the war would be won by then.

The Krits tried projectile artillery but it was useless in the craggy hills. The Rainbow forces suffered few casualties as a result. Krit energy weapons drained too much power for sustained use.

A scanner count at the end of the first day showed 5,678 dead Allorgs, 14 downed aircraft, 164 pieces of heavy equipment scattered along the plains below the hill.

"How accurate is that estimate?" Hodges asked the lieutenant in charge.

She said, "We got all that was showing. I estimate they have at least ten per cent more casualties. Those Allorgs weren't built very well, were they, sir?"

"No, but they got a million of them. Maybe two million to use here eventually. They want this planet."

A sergeant came in, the same beefy sergeant who had smashed the rock. "Good news on all fronts, Colonel Hodges. Minimum casualties. Maximum effect."

"How about our own?"

"Sixty-seven, Colonel," the sergeant said. "I think our ammunition will give before we do."

"Distribute it so we'll last at least another two days."

"Yes, sir. We found two traitors, sir. What do we do with them?"

Hodges took the sergeant aside. "You're sure?"

"No question. They were radioing our positions by pinpoint."

"All right. Kill them. Do it quietly. We don't want to spread alarm."

The sergeant nodded.

"How many wounded?"

"Six."

"Six?"

"They got most of our casualties with energy weapons. They're pretty hot. We don't expect two of them to last the night. We might have to kill the others to prevent the Krits from capturing them."

"I see. Well, get those two traitors taken care of."

Hodges retreated to the back of his cave, telling the lieutenant to disturb him if the Krits made any move at all.

He sat in the lotus position. He was now commanding a little over seven hundred men and women. He needed all the calmness the Circle would bring. Tomorrow, the Krits would put up the strongest drive. Instinct told him that.

He didn't think they would attack at night since his battalion would have the clear advantage. They would attack at dawn. Pinpoint radio indicated that Lester and Charles on the east agreed.

He reflected that war hadn't changed much since the industrialization of mankind, almost a thousand years previously. Eventually, he fell asleep.

The second day proved his instincts to be right. The defenders quickly used their ration of ammunition. Their small cache of energy weapons was exhausted even faster. He was forced to release the last of the ammunition, mostly projectiles. They managed to hold out with 102 killed and 12 wounded.

That evening they heard that the east had fallen and that Lester was hard pressed without much ridge to protect him.

He ordered that documents pertaining to the battle be sealed in rock with him, his six staff officers, and the sergeant only to know the whereabouts.

Hodges also ordered the last of the bullets to be distributed among the troops and officers. Any who wished to could try to make their way to the southern hemisphere. He would order no person to commit suicide. An even sixty made that choice and took the surviving wounded with them.

"What can 556 troops do now, sir?" asked a captain.

"We can hide in these hills and make them come after each one of us. It will tie them up for one more day—one more critical day. . . . Few of us will escape."

The captain nodded. "Six bullets each should mean another three thousand Allorgs dead."

"Go for the Krit officers," Hodges said. "There's a limited supply of them." He took his six bullets and handed one to each of his staff. "I prefer to die my way." He took a sword from his personal belongings. "This is my monking sword. Normally, it would be buried somewhere in the Hobarian desert, but with the foreknowledge that I might fight, I recovered it. It is said that the custom of hiding the sword once it is given by a master to his student came at the end of the war six hundred years ago. It symbolized our dedication to peace. No other person is supposed to ever see it."

"But you show it to us," said the lieutenant.

"There is no peace" was the answer. "During the long peace few swords have been recovered by other than their owners." He held it out for all to see clearly. "A story has it that Liennie, while a student at a university, was on an archaeological expedition with her class and came across a long-rusted sword. It has to have been buried hundreds of years for that alloy to have been rusted. She thought it to belong to Master Gerr, one of the almost legendary founders of Hobar.

"She had been told by her archaeology professor that it was perfectly all right to take swords of obviously dead Hobarians and turn them over to the school museum for identification. They were national treasures and were meant to be shared by all.

"She had a very strong desire to determine whether this skillfully crafted weapon had belonged to the Great Master of the Circle. Besides, it would bring a handsome reward for her then fledgling Ib School.

"Instead, she hid it from the class and reburied it secretly that night where it was unlikely to ever be found again.

"It is very likely that the story is untrue since such an incident would never be made public by Mistress Liennie. Still, it illustrates the importance we of Hobar place upon these swords. You are my comrades-in-arms. It is appropriate for me to share this ancient ritual with all of you."

He had them sit in a circle, his six staff members and the beefy sergeant. He placed the sword on the ground in front of him and kneeled before it. "We of Hobar are not pagans. There is no chant, no prayer, simply a respect for ritual. I hope that you will all sit with me for a while."

Ten minutes later he rose. "Gentlefolks, tomorrow will very likely spell death for us all. Order your forces to spread out over these mountains. If a soldier has a good friend, let that soldier stay with him but see to it that we are spread thin and well hidden. Take a large toll of our enemy. You fight so that future generations of your children and mine will not have to live under the greatest of all tyrannies . . . blind faith."

A report came in the middle of the night that Lester's forces had fallen. Lester and his staff had been summarily executed.

The next morning, 30,000 Allorgs surrounded the ridge where Hodges and his forces were hidden. They were unchallenged in their approach, except for an occasional land mine that had been unexploded up until then.

When they reached the ridge line, a few well-placed traps took care of a few hundred. These were mostly rockfalls. No fire was heard for two hours.

Slowly, as the day wore on, shots were heard. There were a few shouts of men mortally wounded. The Allorgs seemed to have no vocal cords. They died silently, when they died.

Hodges' sword was thick with blood by late afternoon. His coveralls were ripped and he was slightly wounded. He came across the body of the lieutenant. Two Allorgs were dead and she had been repeatedly raped. A few yards away, he saw the bodies of two Krit officers. One had a section of his head missing. The other had been killed with a blow to his face.

The sergeant stood nearby. "I saw what they did," he said over and over again.

Hodges slapped him across the face and ordered him to bury the lieutenant and get on with his job. Then he left to find more Allorgs.

Three were turning a corner. Instantly, two were dead. The third grabbed the colonel's arm. He was thrown and his head removed with a movement of the sword.

Hodges climbed up on a ledge to wait for the officer that would follow.

He came preceded by ten Allorgs. The colonel waited until the androids passed under him and quickly finished off the officer. After that, the Allorgs stood quietly while Hodges cut each of their spinal cords. He moved on. He lost count of how many he killed by early evening. In any case, he was convinced that he had killed sixteen officers.

He used the night to see how many of his own forces were still active. In the middle of the night, he had found three still fighting. He ordered them to go to the southern hemisphere. They had done their job. The 15,000 were as safe now as they could be expected to be.

By first light, thanks to the orderliness of the Krits, he had a fairly accurate count. They had lined up 345 bodies in the plains below the ridge. He estimated a little over one hundred prisoners. He was fairly certain that they would be killed. Such fighters would not be trusted as slave-laborers.

He decided he would hide until dark and then make his way to the southern hemisphere.

He had not counted on aircraft. They simply evacuated the ridge of their own forces and sent out heat-seeking aircraft. There was no fear of their being shot down now. One of the aircraft found traces of his body heat and a section of the ridge evaporated.

Interlude Four: A Coded Message

Ambassador Claymore Chase on Earth and Ambassador Altaire on Svid received the same coded message:

"Rainbow's End has fallen. The Krits are established."

Both men had expected it about the time they received it, and both ordered that the concerned military personnel be informed.

Both were informed that the concerned military personnel had already been informed.

Both men prepared appropriate public statements.

Both said essentially the same thing—that this was expected, that the inhabitants of Rainbow's End had fought with honor and had bought the Confederation time to prepare for the important battles to come, and that a resolution would be presented to the House of Representatives to acknowledge the public debt to Rainbow's End.

Both men said they would introduce private bills to compensate and reconstruct Rainbow's End at the appropriate time.

Liennie on Hobar paid a private visit to the woman with whom Fleet Captain John Hodges had been living for years. She told her and the captain's twelve children that Captain Hodges had not reported after doing the dangerous job of laying mines for Rainbow's End. It was presumed that he died in space.

The woman waited until Liennie had left before she cried.

CHAPTER FIVE

INTERNAL SECURITY

Mr. LaPorte was a small man, barely reaching five feet. He was usually short in an age when nutrition and medicine had insured an average height of six foot three. It was one of those unaccountable genetic things.

As a result, he had been rejected for monitor service in his youth and, to his disappointment, the same records had popped up when he had tried to join the Terran Defense Force only a week previously.

It had been a fortunate accident, he realized, even as he was making his way through the fires and sporatic gunfire of the old section of Nice. A few blocks away, there was an explosion. It shook the buildings he was near, and for a moment he thought one was about to collapse on him.

In his belt, under his jacket, was a fearsome energy weapon. Not fifteen minutes earlier, he had pried it from the hand of a Krit collaborator who must have been killed in a battle days ago. No one had been in the old section to clean it out yet. They had come only to fight.

He had no conception of why he needed this weapon but he thought he should take it . . . as long as it was just lying there.

Mr. LaPorte was a librarian. His full title, for pay purposes, was Assistant Librarian to the Library of Congress, GS-12. He was one of several hundred and, like most of his brothers, the public rarely saw him. An occasional scholar would wander into his section and ask for aid in digging out obscure material. Basically, he was a computer operator very much like thousands of others in all phases of life.

He was a very good computer operator and had a real knack for discovering what was on a particular scholar's mind and getting the right printouts. As a result, he had been transferred to the biotechnology historical section. This section had a reputation for driving librarians to distraction; the average librarian lasted six months.

Not Mr. LaPorte. He saw a real challenge there and happily learned every aspect of his section over the two years he had been there. There was still much to learn.

His supervisor had even secured a small grant for him to compile a guide for fellow librarians before he had barely gotten the suggestion out of his mouth. Two years running he had received the Senate's medal for best civil servant. A token cash prize went with it.

He had been a happy man and had even turned down a promotion to GS-13 knowing that he would have made a poor supervisor.

Then, two months ago, a certain Dr. Melvin Lord came in and asked for a printout on file A-34598.2 Mr. LaPorte gave it to him presuming that the physician had worked on it before and therefore knew the number. He must have lost the original. That sometimes occurred.

Handing him the booklet, fifteen minutes later, Mr. LaPorte noticed that it had a red border, something he had never seen before. He also observed the rare "A" prefix. The lowest category Mr. LaPorte had ever seen started with BZE. He decided that the files were very old.

He jotted down a note to look into it when he had a chance. That would be some weeks hence.

A few days later, he was reading an article in a newspaper that the Krit Embassy staff had left in the last Krit ship to leave Earth. The point of the article was that a serious interstellar crisis was brewing. A list of passengers followed the article, and prominent in the list, because the name didn't follow Krit patterns, was that of Dr. Lord. Later he discovered that Stephen Lock had also left on that ship under an assumed identity.

Mr. LaPorte immediately went to the library, unlocked the staff door, and let himself in. He sat at his console and punched out A-34598.2. Fifteen minutes of impatient waiting followed and at last the red-bordered booklet came out of the printout slot.

He turned the cover. On the inside he read, "Attack biotechnology. This material is MOST SECRET." At first he didn't know what to make of it. He began making a search of who had called for material that might resemble this. Aside from the librarians, no one had handled this section of material in over three hundred years. A librarian had gone through it seventy years before when the new codes were introduced. He discovered that the computer definition of MOST SECRET was a special key signal to release it. That happened to have been disconnected three hundred years previously when one of the scholars complained that it was interfering with his research.

To Mr. LaPorte, biotechnology was entirely an abstraction to be dealt with as a filing system. He knew nothing of its uses except what he read in the press. The word "attack," however, and the obvious Krit collaboration of Dr. Lord made him decide to visit the Army. First, he reattached the special key signal and ordered a superintendent to close off the section, saying he would explain it to his superior the next day.

The army major who listened to his story was polite. He accepted the file and promised to forward it to his superiors. The major told him not to worry. Biotechnology was used to repair damaged organs. True, the Krits were making androids but the Confederation already knew about it and the technology was public knowledge.

His superior felt much the same way but told him that it was his section and he could do what he felt was right.

Mr. LaPorte felt like keeping it closed. On a spark of inspiration, he called for a listing of all "A" material. To his surprise, it was a short list consisting of highly technical data that he could not begin to comprehend. He had a complete printout made. It consisted of 136 booklets which, put within a single cover, were as thick as the length of the librarian's thumb.

He hid the material in the library and again called the army major, who was too busy to see him but assured him that the right people would see the material.

Mr. LaPorte made a decision then that being wartime, certain unorthodox measures were called for. He decided to see Representative Claymore Chase. He still had no idea what he had but he was certain that if the Krits risked taking Dr. Lord aboard, it must have been important.

What Mr. LaPorte didn't realize was that it would take him nearly two months to get through the bureaucracy to see the statesman's aide.

In fact, the aide to Chase told him to bring the booklet before Chase would see him. The booklet was at the library, Mr. LaPorte protested, and the library was in the center of the old section, which was in the heat of battle.

His best chance, the aide said, was to sneak into the library and recover it. The aide had no intention of risking men on a possible chase after an old library book.

So Mr. LaPorte, on the third day of trying, finally reached within two blocks of the library building. He hid, crawled, and ran until he reached the side of the library building. He had heard voices near the entrance so he decided to break a window. Unfortunately, the basement windows weren't glass like the large stately windows that graced the main reading room. It was hard plastic capable of withstanding the pounding of a twenty-pound hammer. He took out the energy weapon and pulled the trigger. Nothing happened.

Mr. LaPorte didn't know that the safety mechanism required the weapon's trigger to be pulled twice the first use in any two-minute wait. He turned it up full not realizing that he could blast a wall with that much power and pulled the trigger again. The window disappeared instantly and he heard explosions on the inside of the building.

He hid behind one of the thousands of statues on the lawn but no one came to investigate. Cautiously, he looked in the window. Automatic fire equipment had already put out the fire. He saw a great deal of destruction and never fully realized that he had caused it.

He entered and went upstairs where the main consoles were

located. He unlocked his section and found the large envelope where he'd hidden the printouts. He turned on his console. Two rows of twenty squares appeared. Without sitting down, he scrambled the key lock to the section with a code he had worked out in his mind just in case the Krits knew the MOST SECRET lock. It would take an expert several weeks to discover the simple code if he died.

He stuffed the envelope into his jacket and left the building the same way he entered.

This time, a Krit collaborator was outside. The bearded man fired his energy weapon at the librarian and hit his left hand, disintegrating it. The librarian dropped, screaming.

The collaborator started walking away, knowing that the little man on the library lawn would probably bleed to death in shock.

But Mr. LaPorte had too much on his mind to allow himself to go into shock. He pulled out his weapon, which was still set too high, and clicked the trigger in the general direction of the collaborator. Nothing happened. More than two minutes had elapsed since the last use. The collaborator turned, weapon in hand.

In a panic, Mr. LaPorte pulled the trigger once more. To his surprise, the collaborator exploded into flames, parts of his body scattering over the avenue. A tree, fifty yards behind the victim, also exploded, and a wall behind the tree collapsed.

Mr. LaPorte hung on to consciousness and his weapon, not realizing that the instrument had exhausted itself of power.

He saw three men running his way, yelling, "We're Terrans!"

He dropped the weapon. Friend or foe, he couldn't see clearly enough to fire.

"Hey, I know this guy," one of the men said. "He's a neighbor from down my block, a librarian."

"Protecting his library when everyone else was hiding," another added.

"Did you see how he blew that collaborator away? Mean for a little guy."

At that point, Mr. LaPorte thought it safe to faint.

A week later, three hundred miles from Earth in a tight orbit, Captain May Mahat sat at her command post in a light cruiser, which, like the other two thousand ships in her fleet, was a converted shuttle. Re-outfitting them with larger engines taking up the former cargo holds had made them fast and efficient and, just as important, capable of extended atmosphere flight. Aircraft were, for the most part, too small and fragile for conversion.

She was returning with her fleet of two-men ships after two weeks of maneuvers. She, like the rest of her fleet, needed training in fighting in outer space. She had made a few mistakes, one costing a life. Her fleet captains had also made mistakes. In all, they lost two ships and five persons.

There was only one thing left to do before she landed.

She turned her head to the Hobarian pilot of her ship and nodded. The man got up and walked over to the assistant commander, an Earther named Igor Stuski. "Sir, Commander Mahat and I would like to make you an honorary member of the Circle since we're all to fight together."

The assistant commander, a former crew chief of the shuttle gang for one of the trading companies, beamed. "I would be honored, Captain."

"Good." The pilot asked the three technicians in the cabin to leave. "We can't have a fancy ceremony as we would on Hobar," the pilot said. "Commander Mahat has some rather bitter fruit juice we use in these ceremonies. Will you serve, Commander?"

Commander Mahat stood and removed a plastic bottle from her coveralls. "We'll all drink from the bottle and the ceremony will be over." She took a sip and passed it to the Hobarian pilot, who also took a sip. With a speed the Earther could not detect, he dropped a grain of chemical into the plastic bottle and gave it to him.

Assistant Commander Stuski took his sip. "That's all there is to it?" he asked.

"We try to keep our rituals simple, sir," the Hobarian pilot said.

"Well, I feel great," said Stuski. He sat in the chair normally assigned to one of the technicians.

"What did you think of the Krits?" Mahat said softly. "I haven't met too many. You, handling cargo, must have met dozens."

"Thousands is more like it," the assistant commander said. "The most arrogant bastards in the universe. Always treated my crews like dirt. Had a good mind to set up a few accidents for them. I always thought some of my crew did but never tried to prove it. Served them right."

He ranted for a few minutes and then recovered from the drug, saying, "What the hell have I been saying?"

"You've been acting out your fantasies," said Mahat. "We have to insure we don't have collaborators abroad. We used a special solution of the powder of the root."

"Me? How could you even suspect me?"

"No one ever suspected Stephen Lock" was Mahat's answer. "I'm sorry. I hope you understand. Each of these ships is equipped with enough power to destroy a city."

Igor Stuski nodded. "You're right, of course."

"With your co-operation, we have to test the rest of the Terrans."

He nodded. "It's too bad, though, that I didn't join your Circle."

"You did," said the Hobarian pilot. "One thing has nothing to do with the other. We'll invite the rest of the Earthers, too."

Igor Stuski smiled.

Captain Mahat invited the technicians in and they went through the same procedure. It was now time for her to land and report to Chase.

There was a ground-car waiting for Commander Mahat when her craft touched down at Nice Outport. The vehicle had no markings. "Considering the recent outbreaks," said the security officer who met her, "we thought it best."

"Why not an aircraft?" Mahat asked.

"We don't know what weapons the collaborators have."

She accepted that and climbed in. A few minutes from the outport, she realized that all was not well. "Stop the car," she ordered.

The driver increased speed. She found the muzzles of two hand pistols in her ribs.

"We're holding the triggers back," said one of the men. "If we let go, we will vaporize you."

"Kill me now," she said.

"No, you will be questioned first, pagan."

Mahat honestly didn't know whether she was quick enough to handle the two men sitting next to her. She considered the possibilities. There were two men in the front of the car and the two sitting next to her in the back. She could reach all four, being almost in the center.

Her master, Avoy of the Albert School, had said to always take care of the weaponless first since those with weapons had slower reaction time. "They have to think for two individuals, themselves and their guns. If you have time, center yourself first."

She had time. She slowed her breathing and knew the position of every muscle in each of her opponents. Suddenly she struck the driver and his passenger. She had moved so fast that when the weapon of the man to her left went off, it struck his partner, whose weapon burned a hole in the back seat. Her left heel broke the survivor's nose. While he was recovering, Mahat had reached the auto button by the driver, and a computer housed somewhere off the highway took control of the vehicle. It slowed to normal speed while she turned and knocked out the survivor. She reached over to the front seat and pulled the driver into the back.

By the time she took the driver's place, the automatic fire-fighting equipment had put out the flames in the back seat and the smell of charred flesh assaulted her. She opened a window slightly, took the car off auto, and increased speed. In the distance, she heard a siren.

Suddenly the car slowed to a stop.

The police had taken control of her car. She hoped they were on her side.

As it turned out they were and, after numerous apologies, they brought her to an old château, the headquarters of Earth's defenses.

"It seems that your maneuvers," said Chase after he had made her comfortable in his own chair, "were mistaken by the collaborators for an attack on Earth."

"I'm sorry," she said.

"Oh, don't be. It couldn't have happened at a better time. An attack of that magnitude by the collaborators while a Krit fleet hung in orbit would have been disastrous. I consider us most fortunate. How did the maneuvers go?"

"Very well. We can now act as one large unit instead of two thousand individuals. I lost two ships through accidents, but we cleared up our communications problems."

He nodded.

"How bad was the attack?" she asked.

"Bad enough," said Chase and depolarized a window. In the early evening light, there was a glow. "That's the old section. Many of the buildings weren't fireproof. They also murdered General Holt and a number of other officials."

"The old section . . ."

"Yes, dear May, including irreplaceable art treasures. This morning, I ordered two thousand killed. I still ponder whether it was my anger or necessity. I've had to order camps built. We're rounding up over a million persons we think fifth columnists.

"I'm an old fool," he continued. "When we discovered Stephen Lock had disappeared, I should have guessed that many of our military men were also Krit agents. It took General Holt's death to convince me. We're doing a thorough housecleaning. There's no room for sentimentality. A hint of suspicion and off the individual goes to a camp. Justice will have to wait for the end of the war. So will apologies. I have around 16 million potential enemies, at least a million of whom are hard core, in a population of 137 million people. If we don't neutralize that element before the real attack, we're in serious trouble."

Captain Mahat walked over to the bar and made Chase the alcoholic drink he favored. "Is there anything I can do?"

"No, it's best that you stay at your duties in space. I've taken the liberty to run a security check on some of your non-Hobarian pilots. You have a number of shuttle pilots being used for orbital defense?"

"Yes, the vast number of them were cargo handlers within the solar system. They're all Earthers. But rest your mind. My people have their own tests. We aren't turning up any Krit sympathizers."

"What are you doing?"

"You've heard of the powder of the root?"

"Oh yes. A drug."

"A very weak solution can give a sane man fantastic visions. He'll live out his fantasies. We are having a number of ceremonies in which we initiate Earth shuttle pilots into the Circle. We think it entirely appropriate since these men and women will be fighting with us and it is understood that after the war, any who wish to drop out can. The initiation is ceremonial in manner since it is unlikely that any of them can be trained in time. They will have the option of joining a Circle school afterward if they choose."

"We introduce a small amount of the powder into their drinks. Initiating three persons at a time, my people question them lightly and lead their imaginations toward Krit dogmas. Most aren't interested. They talk of things such as sexual exploits, their families, even shipping schedules. I doubt that there are any Krit followers in our ranks. The psychologists are right—the religion appeals to the power-hungry and the simpleminded. It has no hold on these technicians, all of whom are well trained."

"Are you sure? They come into contact with more Krits than most people."

"I'm certain. Krits have always treated orbital crews with contempt. The reaction of orbital crews has been contempt in return. The orbital crews, you must remember, also come into contact with more Hobarians than most people. Better than anyone, they've had a chance to compare. Their contempt for Krits is almost institutionalized. I've found the same thing without any elaborate testing with orbital crews around Svid and a dozen other places during my years of moving cargo."

"Drugs aren't foolproof."

She smiled. "Most drugs try to establish facts. That's the reason. The root establishes feelings. You can hide facts but not feelings."

Chase nodded. "Good. Maybe we can clear some of our key people that way. Can you arrange the details?"

"I'll have my aide look into it," she said and thoughtfully added, "Do you think this collaborator trouble is going to hit the other planets?"

"Not on this scale. The Svids are handling it as a minor police problem. They do a little sabotage on some of the minor planets and as far as I can tell, you don't have any collaborators on Hobar. You must understand that Earth is the cradle of all these various world views. The mental attitudes that formed them still appear here and in strength. Heterogeneity is a curse and a blessing at the same time. . . . Now, there's someone I'd like you to meet." He reached for a button. "Send in Mr. LaPorte, please."

The librarian walked in. His left hand was encased in a red oval.

"Mr. LaPorte lost his left hand in honest Confederation service, although no one knew about it at the time. He is a most brave and patriotic man," Chase said for the benefit of Mr. LaPorte, who was feeling nervous in the presence of such august company. "I took the liberty of giving him priority for a bio-grown hand as if he were a frontline soldier, which indeed he was, if unofficially." Chase turned his attention to the librarian. "How long did the doctor say it would take for you to have use of your new hand?"

"At least two weeks, Mr. Representative," the librarian said.

"I'm afraid," said Chase, "that all political offices have been suspended for the duration. Why don't you call me Clay? My friends do." He didn't tell the librarian that that very morning he was named High Commissioner.

"I'm glad to meet you, sir," Mahat said, rising and walking over. She took his right hand and shook it, Earth-fashion.

"Mr. LaPorte is one of our best librarians. He's won many prizes including the Senate medal two years in a row as best civil servant," Chase explained.

"That's wonderful," Mahat said. "Good civil servants make our jobs so much easier." She led the confused librarian to the High Commissioner's chair and gently pressured him to sit down. She went to the bar, prepared him an alcohol drink, and placed it in his hand.

"Don't waste my liquor," Chase said. "Enjoy it."

The librarian took a nervous sip.

"It took Mr. LaPorte two months to reach me through the ponderous bureaucracy I created to keep nuts away. I didn't

realize that it would also keep away honest people like Mr. La-
Porte as well," Chase said and then proceeded to relate the
adventures of Mr. LaPorte in relation to the biotechnology
documents. "I first met Mr. LaPorte three days ago when he
told me what he had discovered. I called a top man in the field
from the University of the Confederation. He took one look at
the procedures in the documents and said, 'biological warfare.' I
nearly fired my aide for making Mr. LaPorte go back for them
alone. If he had been killed . . . well, only the Krit God knows."

"Biological warfare?" Mahat questioned.

"The creation of deadly diseases, very deadly diseases not
found in nature, to use against an enemy. Few people know
that it once existed. The Economic Determinists abandoned it
early in their war. It had a way of turning against them in
unpredictable strains. It was useless as a weapon and lingered
too long."

"These records should have been destroyed centuries ago,"
Mr. LaPorte said, "but I guess librarians can't bear to destroy
knowledge . . . any knowledge. And to think anyone could
have drawn the records by just asking. If some maniac had
asked for them—"

"A maniac did," Chase said, "a whole planet full of maniacs
did."

"I am truly sorry," the librarian said. "If I had only known."

"It's too late for self-blame," Chase said.

"You think they'll use it?" Mahat asked.

"Not on Earth or Svid. That wouldn't serve their purpose.
Mr. LaPorte and I gave this a lot of thought, May. What planet
do they want to completely destroy? What planet were we most
fearful they'd try to use fusion weapons on? What planet do they
hate most?"

"Hobar," she said with a gulp.

Chase nodded and the librarian bowed his head.

"We're certain," said Chase, "that Hobar is in great danger of
being the victim of a lingering biological attack. I'm sending a
team there as soon as you can get me transportation. Mr. LaPorte
has volunteered to go with them. His expertise with a computer
will be most useful. Of course, I'm also warning the other

Confederation planets. We do have one advantage. They only took the attack document and we have all one hundred and thirty-six. We can plan a defense and with incredible good luck, we may be able to avoid a real tragedy."

"Do you think they'll be able to reach Hobar with it?" Mahat said.

"If I asked you to go in a one-man ship and touch Krit's atmosphere, not land, mind you, just touch it and spray a half-ounce of chemicals, could you do it?"

She had to admit that it would be easy.

Chase turned to the librarian and said pleasantly, "Finish your drink. It's good liquor."

Interlude Five: A Letter from Rass to Arlin Elvuse Five Years Before the War

Rass
Technical Institute
Hobar
July 3 (standard)
Turtle 6 (local)

Arlin Elvuse
General Delivery
  or c/o Jewette Lin
Oberland, Svid

Sir Clown:

Professor Lin related your question to me and, I must say, he also sent me a very interesting paper he's written concerning Svid's Clowns.

I can't determine whether his requesting that I reply directly to you is his idea of humor. He can be very subtle and being informed that you were once his student and that your antics have caused some pleasant disruptions of that normally staid planet, I begin to wonder about his motives.

Be that as it may, your question was something to the effect, "How can Hobar produce two such dissimilar persons as Mistress Liennie and Captain May Mahat?"

No doubt you asked the question at the spur of the moment during one of your reputed dialogues with the learned professor. (How I regret never having attended one of these dialogues.)

Still, it is an intriguing question not to be dismissed by the generality that the population is varied on Hobar (though that's true enough).

Let me not be too precise in this. In physics I rank myself with the best. Ask me about the Ctz radical and I'll answer precisely in a few terse sentences. Ask me about human relations and I pale before the most junior student at the Institute. Perhaps if I describe an interesting incident that happened a little over four months ago at Captain Mahat's home, it might clarify some of your thoughts on the matter. I tapped others for some of the information, as I trust their judgment in these matters more than I do mine.

We have a ritual on Hobar that probably predates the settlement of the planet. It's called a tea ceremony. Tea is not used nor is the ceremony anything like the original of ancient Japan (we have pretty good records on that) but we're fairly sure it is derived from it.

It's a fairly important ceremony. If a couple have a tea ceremony with both their sets of parents, they are considered married. The death of a respected family member calls for a tea ceremony (sand is put in the fruit juice on such occasions).

Usually when a master is replaced upon death by his chief assistant, it calls for a tea ceremony given by the new master with the existing students of that Circle school.

The use of the tea ceremony for less formal social occasions has declined over the years. At one time a new business partnership, the birth of a child, and several other minor social events called for the ceremony.

Many reasons are given for the decline. I personally think it's because the traditional drink is too bitter. It comes from a locally grown fruit which originated from the Earth grapefruit. It is little like the grapefruit, however, which is extremely sweet by comparison.

Anyway, it struck all of us as archaic for Captain Mahat to announce her arrival on Hobar after a six-year absence with a tea ceremony. Until the new technology of traveling the vapor universe, it took so long for persons to go to Earth that our representative, Mahat, was away for years at a time. Recent advances now made it possible for her to visit us twice a year. Then there is the recent almost foolproof instantaneous transmission invented by the physicist Keller, of Svid. When we discover a way to make it more private it will certainly be a mixed blessing and not the promised boon.

I was going to decline but was advised by political friends of mine that it might be taken as disapproval of Mahat; not too subtly I was reminded that the Institute derived a good portion of its budget from the House of Representatives, of which she had just become Speaker.

So I went.

The newspapers had talked about it for days. Liennie had accepted as had Avoy of the Albert School, my Circle master. There were a number of persons also invited with whom you would not be familiar, Sir Clown.

The social gossips in our newspapers (an assortment of persons Svid is blessed in not having) spoke for days about the seating order. There was no question that Liennie would occupy the place of honor to the right of Mahat. But who was to be on the left? Avoy was Mahat's Circle master and I was her superior in the Fleet. Then there was the problem that Avoy was also my Circle master.

It amazes me how these trite things can occupy so much newspaper print. Probably the only ones totally unconcerned were Liennie, Avoy, and myself.

There's a rumor that Liennie sent Mahat a note giving her space up for me. I know Avoy did the same. I was a little mischievous and didn't send a note. I know that she would have graciously accepted mine. I wanted to see what Mahat would do.

We all entered the tea ceremony a few moments late, as custom demands, in the flowing robes that tradition demands. I was enjoying the predicament totally. Besides, I would finally meet Liennie for the first time. I was in high spirits.

Mahat placed Liennie in the position we thought Mahat would occupy, Avoy to Liennie's right and me to her left. Mahat took the last chair at the table leaving everyone a little baffled.

There's this legend, probably the construction of some storyteller, that a number of notables of the Circle in Master Gerr's original school were fighting for the place of honor at a tea ceremony. The situation threatened to erupt into a violent argu-

ment. Gerr is supposed to have taken the lowest position at the
table and his students then understood their stupidity.

Mahat had done an intelligent thing and I felt a little stupid
in forcing the situation.

It did show me what a fantastic politician Mahat was, and
that night I was inclined to forget my disagreements with her.
She had introduced several bills to irritate the Krits. I never
could understand her total dislike for them. As badly as they
behave, I had always presumed that they had freedom to live
the way they wanted.

In the quadro-centennial polls of the Confederation, the people of Krit had given their form of government a total backing.
This could not be said for the other planets.

Mahat had only said that it proved that the Krit people had
no real choice and called on the Confederation for a recon-
stitution of their government. Mahat was a political realist on
many matters. Not on this one, I judged. My political friends
agreed.

I always considered her dangerous to the general peace, but
that night I was perfectly willing to enjoy the presence of
everyone, including Mahat.

Now, there is the red spoon, another part of the ceremony.
(If all these details bore you, Sir Clown, skip the next few para-
graphs.) The person with the red spoon initiates the conversation. Dozens of books specify who is to get it and in what order.
The usual story was that in the early days when egos were high,
the master of the ceremony would put it by the glass of his
favorite and he would have undisputed authority in the conversation.

Naturally, Liennie found it in front of her. She smiled and
immediately passed it to Avoy, her senior if less legendary figure.
Avoy returned it and Liennie passed it to me.

I could almost see Mahat swallow as the honored instrument
began making the rounds of the eight guests, each returning
it to Liennie. Finally, she passed it to Captain Mahat and, of
course, Captain Mahat had to return it as much as she would
have liked to keep it. She had gathered the group for some
reason.

Another interesting thing about the ceremony was the immaculate order in which everything was arranged. Every detail had been seen to, even to the spreading of leaves around the tea house. I suppose this is possible when one owns his own tea house. Few people can afford this anymore. I myself hire a commercial tea house when I need a tea ceremony, as I'm sure most people do.

A person like Liennie very probably converts a common room.

The immaculate order struck me as unnecessary and showed a lack of understanding on the part of Captain Mahat. There's something spiritual about the ceremony and order belongs to science, not the spirit. Even the grossest of commercial tea houses understands this and the more human a tea house can be without shattering the image of spirituality, the more successful it is.

But it had escaped Captain Mahat's understanding. The place looked like the ideal as illustrated in *Mot's Book of Ceremonies*, which my mother had shown me as a child. She must have planned it for days. "A well-ordered tea house reflects the owner's purpose. If the owner means to use his guests, everything will be perfect so perfection should be avoided. The tea ceremony should be social and spiritual. For business, call a business conference." (Mot, Chapter 6.)

Mahat must have skipped that chapter.

Liennie, on the other hand, always gave the impression that she never once read a book. She fitted anywhere. I'm told that this is one of the true indications of mastery of the Circle.

(Don't misunderstand, Liennie reads heavily. Her mind is as sharp as yours or Professor Lin's. Once, she announced that the Ctz radical was the center of the universe, or the *Chi*, in the old Chinese concept. She had made an unfortunate simplification common to people who do not absolutely understand the dangers of such simplification—that is, nonscientifically trained individuals.

It was doubly dangerous because she would be listened to and it might put pilots in danger if they blindly accepted this idea.

I wrote her a letter explaining how she was mistaken and

explaining the effect her statement might make on budding pilots. I also enclosed a long lecture on proper scientific thinking and how simplification can be used effectively.

To her credit, she took my letter, which I'd intended as a private warning, and made it public with her endorsement. She stated that she had been wrong and added that all matters concerning the Ctz radical on which she might be consulted would be referred to the Institute.

Later, we had a long conversation by phone on the Ctz radical. She had grasped completely all I had told her.)

But to return to the tea ceremony. There was a long silence while Mahat, acting out the lowest role, poured the juice. We sipped it ceremoniously and silently. Master Avoy then took from under the table his yin-yang, a musical instrument, and Liennie took out her flute. They played for some two hours while the rest of us allowed ourselves to go into a minor meditative state. I sensed that Mahat listened politely only.

It was beginning to be apparent that Liennie had no intention of initiating a conversation. As a major spiritual leader, it was her option to ignore tradition. I was delighted and half-amused.

When they put their instruments down, Liennie said, "I understand that Captain Mahat is a mistress of the Earth musical instrument, the guitar. I would certainly enjoy hearing her play."

The guitar is not a traditional instrument of the tea ceremony but Liennie is a great spiritual leader. Mahat had to go out of the tea house and get her guitar.

"Play something melodic," Liennie softly instructed the politician.

After half an hour, I found myself tapping in time. Mahat was a good musician. I also noticed that the tension left her. She relaxed totally as she continued to play.

Then Master Avoy joined in. For three hours, he played with her. Liennie joined in and added her very real talents. I was asked to play the Liv drum, a dullard's instrument which can be learned in a few minutes. At around four in the morning, everyone was deep into playing music, some doing little more than tapping a glass with their spoon.

With the first dawn, an hour later, people drifted out.

It had been a very successful ceremony. Mahat was in very excited spirits. She had forgotten for a few hours that she was a politician. It had been good for her soul.

Outside the house, Liennie asked Mahat, "May I stay at your home for some sleep? It is a long journey to Ib Village."

"I have a mat prepared for you, sister," Mahat said.

"When we wake, in a few hours," Liennie said, "perhaps we can discuss politics. I need to know your views on certain matters." Liennie walked away, led by a servant to her bed.

I was nearby. I saw Mahat's face immediately transform itself back to that of the politician. All the tension returned.

I was really feeling sadness for her. Liennie had never intended to avoid the discussion of politics with Mahat but had, in her kindness, taken the burden from Mahat for a night. I don't think Mahat understood, however.

Well, I don't know if I've really answered your question, Sir Clown, but perhaps I've been able to show you how our interrelations work. I think that's useful.

If you feel inclined, write me a letter.

Give my best to Professor Lin.

Faithfully,
Rass

CHAPTER SIX

THE ALLORGS

Nevin Baze balanced the energy weapon in his hands. It was light empty and not very heavy when charged. It was a new weapon, probably off the assembly line only a few days. It felt comfortable already.

"Hey, Baze," said his neighbor lying in the next bunk, "thinking how many Krits you're going to kill?"

Nevin let a grin grow on his face. "I've never had a gun like this."

"Don't let the sergeant hear you call it a gun. It's a weapon. I got a gun. Must be two hundred years old. I think it was used to kill birds. It'll never stop one of those Allorgs."

Somebody from across the barracks yelled, "Shoot him in between the eyes. It can't move without a brain."

"You sure that's where the brain is?" the neighbor asked.

There was laughter.

In the lottery to determine who was going to have the one energy weapon allowed this squad, the neighbor had won but he had said, "I'm two hundred pounds," and had given it to Nevin who was only sixteen (standard) and somewhat lighter.

"You think they'll have more weapons before we go tomorrow?" Nevin asked.

"No," his neighbor said pointedly. "They're hard to manufacture and we're in a hurry. Anyway, who told you we were going tomorrow?"

"Talk," Nevin said.

"We go when that guy, Shear, says we go," his neighbor said, "and he isn't talking."

A man from across the aisle said, "Think we can trust the Hobarians?"

The neighbor, older than the others, nodded. "They got to go in first and soften them up. When they decide to commit us, they'll be ready, don't you worry. Those boys are cautious as hell."

"So why are we going without everybody having an energy weapon?" the same man asked.

The neighbor, who was growing tired of the exchange, said, "Because there aren't enough to go around. You want to sit around for another two months?"

The door to the barracks slid open and the sergeant walked in, followed by a Hobarian pilot. The sergeant looked around. "Don't you men stand up in the presence of an officer?"

The eight men in the squad quickly got to their feet.

"All right, relax," the sergeant said. "Commander Rone has a few things to say to you."

Nevin looked at the pilot. He had never seen a Hobarian close up before because he came from a small city without an outport. The Commander seemed far different from television pictures. His coveralls were loose-fitting. In fact, you could see his neck and half his chest. He was much older than Nevin imagined pilots to be but that may have been because his head was shaved. Without the makeup television provided when one of these individuals was interviewed, Nevin could see that his face was pock-marked with radiation burns. His eyes were certainly bios. It was said that the average pilot needed to replace them at least twice in a lifetime.

The captain looked around and he noticed Nevin staring at him. He smiled and said gently, "I'm not as ugly as the Allorgs you'll meet."

The squad laughed.

The Commander turned to the whole group and produced a small bottle from his pocket. "We'll be fighting together very soon, gentlemen. Though I'll be in space and you'll be on land, it will be important that we co-ordinate everything we do, so our squadron here on Svid voted to invite any of the soldiers who wish to become honorary members of the Circle. We wish we had time to train each and every one of you before the upcoming battle, but that is impossible. We promise, though, that after the war, we will set up centers so that those who want to can become true Circle brothers. In the meantime, this small ritual will enable us all to call each other brother as well as comrade."

He opened the bottle and took a small sip and passed it to the next man, Niven. "It's very bitter," he said. "Just take a sip."

Niven did and passed it to his neighbor.

The whole thing took little more than five minutes and Commander Rone left after saluting the men in the Hobarian manner, the right fist in the left hand. The sergeant followed.

Niven's neighbor returned to his bunk. "I think you're right, Niven. We leave tomorrow."

The man across the aisle said, "That Commander Rone is our squadron leader. He behaves like a general, at least."

"He doesn't look like a general," Nevin said.

"You're right about that," his neighbor agreed, "but he thinks like one. We're in good hands."

Dr. Margaret Moore hadn't had much sleep since returning to Svid. She and Commander Lor Rone had just returned from Allorg where they had secretly raided a factory producing androids. They had brought back several of the huge Allorgs but had been unable to secure Allorgs in their natural state.

This disturbed her and she said as much to Commander Shear, who was sitting across the table from her. "If we destroy the plants we run the risk of destroying the species. We have no members of that species to clone a new population from. We should have risked staying."

Shear was contemplative and said, "I appreciate the problem, Doctor, but you had no choice. Without the Allorgs you brought back, our army wouldn't have known what they were up against. It might have made a decisive difference. I've instructed our ground forces as well as the pilots on the bombing runs to hit the buildings only. We're fairly certain that there are plenty of Allorgs in the natural state to replenish the planet. You yourself said that they only needed a half-dozen males to produce their army by cloning."

"Commander," she objected, "the plants were all on one subcontinent. That's a sure indication that the Allorgs are small in numbers. A heavy bombing raid could destroy them all."

"Doctor, I've already assured you that we won't be using fusion weapons. But we can't wait. Another month and they'll have the estimated six million androids off-planet. Now, you went over the figures with us. We know that they've bought enough chemicals in the last ten years to create that many once they had the genetic patterns, and they must have had them within a year of starting the project. The estimate is six million. If they deploy that many, the Confederation will fall. I've barely seventy thousand troops to fight them with."

The biologist was still disturbed. "Why did we sell them the chemicals?"

"Who knew that war was coming?" he retorted. "There are thousands of honest uses for the same materials."

She knew it was hopeless. "With your permission, Commander, I want to go along. If you assign me some men, I'll make an attempt to save two Allorgs in their natural state."

"I admire your humanity, Doctor. As much as I hate to risk endangering you, I have to grant your wish. I think that with the cover of battle, you might just get away with it. I'll see to it that you get an experienced pilot to fly a small fast ship, one of the new design. He should be able to sneak your squad in and out quickly."

"Will it be Captain Rone?"

Shear shook his head. "He's a Commander now and he's more useful leading the bombing raid. Why don't you go to your quarters and get some sleep? I know that you've worked hard compiling the data for the troops in the last few days. The campaign begins tomorrow so get your equipment ready."

"Tomorrow?"

Shear nodded. "It's a secret to keep to yourself."

She returned to her quarters at the university and shut the door.

Being a large compound, the university had been transformed as one of three staging areas for the coming push. Hundreds of men and women of the newly formed service were quartered on the once quiet suburban campus.

Dr. Moore was forced to close her door, although once it had been open to anyone who wished to consult her. The place was littered with books since her student aide had left to join the new army. She cleared several thick volumes from the newly installed cot and lay down. A title had caught her eye. It was one of the books she had promised herself to read. She let herself get absorbed in it.

Two hours later, there was a knock on her door.

The man she let in was Commander Rone.

"You seem relaxed on the eve of battle," he said.

"It's a two-week journey to Allorg," she answered.

"Not for you," he answered. "You'll be in suspended animation. It'll be like a day. Peer told me what you propose to do. You're a courageous person.

"It's necessary" was her answer.

"Yes, it is," he agreed. "I just dropped by to tell you that your pilot will be Dalka Myron. I picked him myself. He's had thirty years' experience. He was a pilot before this new vapor universe was discovered so you know he's one of the best. He's one of the calmest men I know and a master of the Circle . . . a true master."

"Thank you."

Rone looked at her. "Look, I know that you're upset that I forced you to leave before you could get your natural Allorgs, but I had very specific orders. Captain Myron will also have specific orders. He is to see to it that you get your specimens regardless of risk."

"Can I be sure of that?"

"Yes, there's no military necessity in his pulling out quickly as there was for me. I had to get androids back. Our people had to know what they were fighting. These Allorgs are very different from the ones who attacked Rainbow's End. These are fairly independent. Can you imagine the harm it would have caused if we had gone on the assumption that they had to be controlled by a Krit officer, as reported in that last Keller transmission from Rainbow?"

"I understand," she said in an indifferent tone. "Yet I know that you had planned on bombing Allorg anyway, so what was the use?"

"Dear lady, I'm going to land two thousand men to mop up Allorg. We are also going to strike Mora's World and Rainbow simultaneously. They may not have needed complete androids to fight that ragtag army on Rainbow's End, but now they do. We had to know."

"I'm sorry," she said. "The idea of wiping out Allorg, which may someday have a civilization like ours, simply upsets me. I have to save those primates."

"And we'll do everything we can to help," he said.

"I know you will," she said. "Forgive me."

He smiled at her and took out a packet. "These are the reconnaissance photos we took on our first orbit three weeks ago. I don't know whether they'll help but maybe they will. Stay away from the red area I've outlined. That's where we'll be bombing. You'll have about seventy-two standard hours to round up your specimens. A special star ship will meet you at a rendezvous. Captain Myron will have the details on that."

"Three days?"

"We have no plans to hold Allorg. It would take more men than we can spare and it has no military value once the plants are destroyed. We have to hold Mora's World and Rainbow's End. That's where the bulk of our forces will be striking. Besides, if you're there more than three days, you're certain to be discovered because we'll be gone. They'll have nothing better to do than search for you."

She opened the packet and started going through the blowups. The military used the photographs to look for artificial buildings. She was using them to look for vegetation and rivers. In an instant, she found three likely spots. She marked them and returned the photographs to Captain Rone. "This is where I want Captain Myron to land, in the order I marked them."

"I'll see that he gets them."

"And can I get some of those heat sensors I've heard about? I understand they can be tuned for animal temperature."

"They're already on your ship with a few other gadgets we thought you could use. A sergeant Lans, who will lead your squad, can fill you in. By the way, you're a lieutenant for the mission. It'll make it easier for you to handle your men."

She smiled as he handed her the star she was to wear on her collar. He apologized for having to leave immediately and she returned to her book.

Nevin Baze was as confused as the rest of the squad when Sergeant Lans handed each man an energy weapon. "All I know," the sergeant said, "is that we're on special assignment. Get your gear. We're supposed to meet with some professor or other."

The men piled into the back of a truck once used to move perishables and were driven across the campus to the university staff offices. They passed dozens of individuals in the hallways and were led into a room with books piled all over the floor.

A Hobarian and a woman were waiting.

Sergeant Lans closed the door and suddenly everything was silent. The room was soundproof.

The Hobarian said, "Find yourselves places to sit down." He waited while the group made themselves comfortable and said, "You're all on special assignment. It'll be away from the main combat but will possibly be as dangerous. Maybe not. If anyone wants to stay with the main force for whatever reason, leave now."

No one stirred.

"Very well. From now on, we will all stay together. Any loose talk could put us in serious danger. We leave in two hours and will lay over in our ship until the entire force assembles. Our assignment is Allorg like the rest of the squadron, and until we reach the Allorg star, we will remain with the group for protection and cover. As soon as we reach the star, we leave the group and make our way by separate course to the planet. Our mission will best be explained by Dr. Moore."

The thin dark-haired woman spoke. "We're on a mission of

mercy. It may be the most important thing to happen in this war. While the squadron destroys the android factories, we will attempt to save two Allorg primates in their natural state. One of each sex. If we should destroy the subcontinent they thrive on, we will be able to start the species again, by laboratory means. As I'm sure you've read or heard, many scientists think that they may be the start of another galactic civilization. For us to not save them would make us no better than the Krits who violated the Allorg ban. We have to try."

She produced a six-foot picture of an Allorg warrior. "This android was biologically produced from this." She put a picture of an Allorg male over the other picture. "This is his true size. Notice that he does not stand erect and is covered with hair. The nose is very much like that of a baboon. He is a grass eater, according to the expedition that first studied him, and very shy. Still, he is faster than you are so that several of you with nets may be necessary to trap him."

She produced another picture. "This is the female. Notice the two spots on her nose. It's a sure sign that she's the female. We need one of each. Don't climb a tree after them but call for help. The tree is where they travel fastest."

Nevin raised his hand. To Dr. Moore's nod, he asked, "You mean they produced those warriors from those?"

She nodded. "Yes. We know that their first production was incomplete. They were in a hurry to capture Rainbow's End. They've improved the lot to think independently—not as well as you do but sufficiently to follow orders blindly."

The Hobarian interrupted. "Your squad ship will be attached to the first wave. I will be piloting that control. As soon as we hit normal universe, I will leave the control, detach the squad ship, and fly you direct. We'll be out of the area before the Krit defenses can attack. Our ship will be crowded. It's not a large shuttle but an especially designed scout. Unfortunately, it was designed to accommodate five men comfortable, not eleven. Besides that, we have to have three extra suspended-animation chambers, in case we catch more than two of the species so you will enter your chambers immediately on boarding and I won't wake you until we're an hour out of Allorg. Any questions?"

No one had any.

"Very well, gentlemen. There's a truck waiting downstairs for us. Please pick up the baggage stacked by the door as you leave. Dr. Moore and I will follow in a few moments."

"Should we hold the truck for you, sir?" Sergeant Lans asked.

"Please do," said the pilot. He closed the door behind them and turned to the biologist. "Have you been initiated into the Circle, Doctor?"

She shook her head. "I'm afraid I've never really followed those things much."

"May I invite you, madam?"

"I'd be honored, Captain Myron. Hobar is all those things I've admired for years. I've just never had the opportunity, although I've wanted to look into it."

"The Circle is not an intellectual exercise, but it helps the mind," he reassured her.

She nodded.

"Stand in front of me," the captain said, "and give me both your hands."

Interlude Six: Excerpted From
The Child's Book of the Confederacy

Distances: It is clumsy to say Earth is 6,890 light-years from Hobar. It is much easier to say that Earth is 234.6 standard hours from Hobar since hours are the measure used by commerce. A few years ago, before the new discoveries in traveling faster than light, Earth was 1.9 standard years from Hobar. Though the physical distance actually enlarges as the universe expands, the Confederacy is actually growing smaller as our ships get faster. In 6,700,000 standard years, the universe will have changed its wave relationship with the vapor universe we now use to travel so that once again, Earth will be 1.9 standard years from Hobar. Scientists believe that the wave relationship between our universe and the newly discovered vapor universe only became compatible 170 years ago but it took us all that time to discover it. (For more information, see the listings: *Universes, Relativity,* and *Ctz radical.*)

The Allorgs: Inhabitants of the planet Allorg discovered over two hundred years ago by the explorer, Alan Larly. They are the closest form of life ever discovered closely relating to our own. It is believed that they may one day evolve into a civilization similar to ours and to insure that possibility, the Allorg ban was voted by the House of Representatives sitting in special session. Each planet took an oath to keep the ban.

CHAPTER SEVEN
THE TRIANGLE STRIKES ALLORG

The ship's chronometer had gone haywire again—the second time it had done so during the trip. This didn't disturb Commander Rone. It was one of those things that happened in the vapor universe.

His internal clock knew that there were thirteen minutes to transference.

When he broke from the vapor universe, he would be within a half mile of the scheduled point of break. He checked the energy lines that held the seventy pods together. The instruments he needed for that were also out of kilter but they said enough to assure him. In front of him were the star maps for the area. Astro-navigation was more important to him at that moment. He had been to Allorg only once and he wanted to make sure that the fourth planet from star G-987 would be where they told him it would be. He used a mechanical slide rule rather than the unreliable computer.

The rule, in the vapor universe, was that as long as it didn't involve electricity, it was safe to use. Men used electricity to live biologically and his own pet theory was that Circle meditation kept it at a level that was usable so that Hobarians didn't go mad.

Of course, that didn't explain how the Krits did it. They had no Circle meditation or, for that matter, any form of meditation. Besides, his theory was wrong and had, in his lifetime, been demonstrated to be wrong. Still, he held on to it. What was the difference what the rationale was if it worked?

The seventy pods were spaceships intended for interplanetary travel, mostly converted shuttles, each containing twenty-five troops and equipment.

The other two controls, which would approach Allorg on the same side of the sun as the planet, had as pods the bombers containing no soldiers. It was hoped that they would attract all the attention while he approached from the other side of the sun from the planet's position. They would bomb first and his ships would land two hours later and mop up. The old books had emphasized mopping up as bombers usually left too much standing.

As soon as the pods left the three controls, the controls would re-enter the vapor universe on a preset course for Svid. It was unlikely that they would be recovered since without a human pilot, too much could go wrong. However, controls were costly and even a remote chance of recovery was worth the effort.

After the raids, the ships would meet new controls at rendezvous points. These controls would have dummy pods to coincide with the expected weights of the returning ships. If a fighting ship didn't return, the controls would simply keep one of the dummies.

The reason for this clumsy operation was that controls had to be exactly balanced as far as mass was concerned in order to operate properly. It took a week of precise calibration to balance a ship and no one was willing to wait a week with an enemy fleet at their heels. Besides, in the normal universe, controls were slower than ordinary ships and would probably be destroyed while they lay in wait for the returning fighters unprotected. That chance couldn't be taken. Lives were at stake.

The operation was clumsy but it would work, in theory. No one was guessing how the Krits were doing it.

A large cash prize was offered by the combines which owned the expensive controls to anyone who could think of anything better. But by battle time, no one had thought of anything. Later in the war, someone would figure out how to calibrate a control in seconds. But most of the battles would have been fought by then and there would be no need for such speed in moving cargo.

A minute before break-out time, Commander Rone took his position. At the precise instant, he pressed the sphere. The lights disappeared for an instant and he was once again in normal space.

Now he had to work fast.

He immediately sent the wake-up signal to the warships orbiting his control and then scanned the immediate space for possible Krit defenders.

There was a patrol consisting of three ships, twenty minutes away. He surmised that there was plenty of time. Only ten minutes were needed to get the pods under way.

Within three, he was signaled by the pod commanders that they were awake. He broke the holding field and set the autopilot. Then he himself left the control for his own pod and left it to disappear five minutes later into the vapor universe.

His pod had three subcommanders and he woke them up immediately after breaking orbit of the control. The other pods, now turned troop ships again, would wait until an hour out of Allorg before waking their troops. In space, the troops would be of no use except to get in the pilot's way.

Eight light-hours on the other side of the sun, Captain Dalka Myron took control of the light bomber after his control went into the vapor universe. The attack squadron was well on its way and he took a silent path on another vector with his party.

The Krits had dispatched a force after them and a dogfight ensued. The Krits had come out rather poorly and withdrawn to lick their wounds. Myron suspected that the Krit commander had spread his forces thin and mostly as a warning line. Of the fifteen ships that tried to hit his force of sixty-six, three limped away and one was hot on his tail and would likely catch him in an hour.

Though Myron had promised Dr. Moore, reluctantly at the last minute, to awaken her immediately, he had no intention of doing so until he disposed of the swift Krit ship behind him.

Myron also suspected that the bulk of the Krit force was in

orbit around the planet and that a more serious fight would occur, probably with casualties on the Triangle side this time.

As to his pursuer, it gave him cause to worry. It was obviously a one-man cruiser made up mostly of engine so it was faster and more maneuverable. But its Krit pilot, if he followed the norm, would prefer a confrontation to trickery. Most people who were fanatics were like that. Myron didn't intend to play his game. He didn't even intend to wait until the Krit got within range when he would be more alert.

He dropped a small mine, about six inches in diameter, of a fusion variety. If the Krit was enough of an idiot to follow him directly and got within three miles of the now dormant mine, it would be enough.

Twenty minutes later, Myron discovered that his adversary was an idiot.

He woke up Dr. Moore.

She was groggy, not being used to suspended animation as a seasoned traveler might be.

"Take your time, Doctor. We're sixteen hours out of Allorg, relative time. This ship isn't as fast as a control."

"Are we in danger?"

"No. We managed to disperse from the emergence point without serious difficulty. The problems will begin when we hit Allorg."

She staggered about a little. "Is this what you warned me about?"

He nodded. "Even near-light speed affects you. Just relax and don't fight it. Sleep if you like."

"I have work to do," she said, repeating the argument she had given him for waking up early.

"Go about it slowly and you'll get it done," he advised her. He lay back in the control seat. "I'm going to sleep for a few hours. Wake me if you don't feel well and I'll reset your cocoon."

"Suppose we're attacked?"

"Unlikely. Besides, the automatic equipment is faster than I could be in spotting an enemy. There's an alarm system." He polarized the front port. In an hour, it would be facing the blinding sun.

Dr. Moore spent most of the sixteen hours checking and re-checking her equipment. She sat in the copilot's seat and fell asleep once she was satisfied.

Captain Dalka woke about three hours out of Allorg. This was near the critical time when an attack might be expected. He would have to restart the engine soon and his ship wouldn't be as invisible to being spotted. He glanced at the sleeping Dr. Moore and decided not to disturb her.

He depolarized the port which was now facing ninety degrees from the sun and tried to guess where the Krit fleet might be. The rest of the strike force should be turning on their engines about then and he was scheduled to turn on twenty minutes later in the hope that the Krits would have been sufficiently distracted by the two strike fleets to miss his lone ship.

Of course, there was no way for him to know what was going on. His scanners were set for ten minutes away. Anything more than that might attract unwelcome visitors. As soon as he turned on the engines, however, he would be able to set to full range. Engines were more attracting than scanners.

As soon as the engines went on, the scanners told him that there was a full-blown battle around the planet. They also told him that no one had spotted him.

Dr. Moore woke up. "How long have I been sleeping?"

"You were asleep when I woke up, Doctor, an hour ago. Did you accomplish what you wanted?"

"Yes," she said. "Are we still traveling fast?"

"Not very fast. Our relative time has slowed fairly close to normal. You wouldn't be able to tell the difference without a sensitive chronometer." He smiled. "You can speak to the Krits if you like."

"No thanks," she said, returning the smile.

"We're two hours out of Allorg," Captain Dalka said. "There's quite a battle going on with the two bomber squadrons."

"Where?"

"About a hundred thousand miles at ten o'clock." He pointed but nothing could be seen except small sparks of light. "That's a ship going boom. I hope it's one of theirs." He turned on the radio receiver.

"Lan, 360!" voices from the speaker said. "Eight o'clock! Spread this one! Hsss. Nine o'clock! Six coming. Widen the formation! Sit on him! Good going. Watch it, Miles! Stay with Lort, Davis! Jump on him, Lort! Davis, stay tight! Hsss. Mary, get that stray! Davis, Krit on Mary's tail. Get him!"

Captain Dalka listened intently. Dr. Moore was silent.

"Davis, Mary's crippled, stay with her! Mary, you all right?"

"Yes," she said. "No power."

"Davis, cover her and mark the course. We'll pick her up after the run."

"No good," said another voice. "She'll hit planetside in fifteen seconds."

"Mary, get out! Davis, pick her up!"

"Door's fused . . . hsss."

Captain Dalka turned the receiver off. "Mary Wilson and I attended the Institute together. She was the other squadron leader."

"Do you resent this assignment? Would you rather be with them?"

Captain Dalka shook his head. "It has to be done. I'd better wake the squad." He left the seat and walked to the rear of the compartment.

Dalka's ship swung a sharp parabola toward the south pole. Commander Rone had come in that way before to pick up the Krit warriors and hadn't been spotted. There was a great deal of magnetic interference there. Like Rone before him, he flew low, at less than one thousand feet and headed for the delta where Dr. Moore thought they might pick up natural Allorgs.

He landed the ship gently, while Sergeant Lan prepared his men. Nevin Baze was instructed to stick with the ship while the party walked the three miles to the delta headwaters.

An hour after the party left, Baze began to get nervous. He heard explosions to the south, and although he guessed correctly that it was the android factories being attacked, he was still nervous.

Occasionally, he would see a craft fly high overhead at great speeds. He even saw one explode and never knew whether it was friend or foe.

He breathed a sigh of relief when the party radioed in to say by a brief code word that they were staying outdoors for the night.

Baze followed instructions and closed the lock before going to sleep that night. It was hours before he finally fell asleep. He was in a slight panic. Only a month before he had been in the comfort of his parents' home thinking about the trade he would eventually enter.

Now, he was on a strange planet, in a ship full of weird lights. It was a ship he did not understand. It seemed as if there was a barrier between him and the walls. He feared touching a wrong button. The pilot had neglected to tell him that the ship was "locked" to his touch. Baze could sit on the buttons for all it mattered.

He lay back in the pilot's couch feeling the strange plastic on his neck and hands. He guessed that they had left him behind because he would not be much use in a fire fight. If the ship was attacked without the pilot being present, it would make little difference that he was there. Svid attitudes, he knew, still saw him as being at a clumsy and unreliable stage of life.

He knew how to operate the radio but what use would that be in saving the ship—and without the ship, their little squad was doomed.

But eventually he fell asleep.

About two hours later, the ship's buzzer went off. Someone was approaching the ship. He fumbled for the energy weapon and held it tightly in his hand.

The radio speaker came to life. "Baze, this is Dalka. I'm coming from the south. Open the lock and be prepared to cover me! Three Allorg warriors are in hot pursuit and a hell of a lot faster than I am."

The youth rushed to the lock and opened it. He held his weapon tightly and peered to the south. Barely, he could make out a running figure carrying something. Close behind were three larger figures.

"Dalka, get out of range!" he found himself yelling.

The first figure stepped to the side and Baze found himself firing wildly in the general direction of the Allorgs.

The ground around the androids exploded in lights. It took intense seconds for all three to go down and Baze kept firing even when they no longer moved.

Dalka had circled and was almost to the ship when Baze heard him say, "Don't waste energy! They're gone!"

He stopped firing and jumped from the lock. He accepted the body Dalka had been carrying. It was Dr. Moore. It took him a second to realize that the Hobarian's right arm was missing and that the man was in extreme pain.

"Put her in a cocoon and press the green button. She's not dead, but just barely. Let's hope that the suspended animation will freeze the life in her."

Baze obeyed without question. He lay the biologist in the cocoon, closed it and pushed the button while the pilot closed the lock. He rushed to the control couch and began pressing buttons.

Baze turned just as the artificial gravity flipped on. They were airborne. "What happened?" Baze said, sitting in the co-pilot's seat.

"We ran into a patrol. The squad was in the front. Get the medical kit behind the seat! Lost blood."

Baze jumped up and got it. He opened it.

"See the green canister? Follow the instructions. Spray my right arm."

It took Baze long seconds to read it, and finally, he sprayed the arm at the stump near the shoulder.

Dalka was breathing heavily. "I lost too much blood. I'll never make it to the rendezvous. I've preset the course and taped the code. When you reach rendezvous, you'll be challenged. Press this button and a radio channel will open. Tell them the pilot is in a cocoon and you need help. Someone will come and place the ship where it belongs."

Dalka looked at him. "Listen carefully! I have to leave the controls unlocked. Do not . . . I repeat, do not touch them no matter what happens. If you go off course, you'll never meet rendezvous. If the Krits blow you out of space, you're better off than lost. Take my word for it. If they challenge you, don't reply. If they try to enter the ship, press this green button. It'll evaporate the ship. I can't chance their knowing the rendezvous point or getting the code. They'll kill you regardless, so die with pride and save your comrades!"

Baze nodded gravely.

Dalka smiled. "Now, help me to a cocoon."

Dalka closed his eyes. He was dead.

Baze was sure he was dead but couldn't take even a small chance. He struggled with the much heavier body and managed to put it in a cocoon and freeze it.

Nevin Baze encountered no Krit ships and his ship was re-covered with the survivors of the two squadrons and the surviving troops. On the return to Svid, he would discover that casualties had been heavy but 80 per cent of the androids had been destroyed before they could get off planet.

The assault would be called successful.

Interlude Seven: Excerpted From
The Child's Book of the Confederacy

Krit: Fourth planet from star G-98764. Colonized before the War
of the Economic Determinists and not touched by that war.
Its origins are obscured by legends. According to the Krit
Embassy, a man named Lazarus and his four wives, who said
they were simple farmers, first touched down on the planet
after having purchased space on a pioneer explorer-class ship.
They are said to have built up the planet aided by some
miracles from the Krit God. Other sources think this theory
to be far-fetched. They suggest that the Krits are the remains
of some exotic religions of old Earth and that a number of
individuals were involved. But whether the original colonists
consisted of five individuals or a thousand, the accomplish-
ments of Krit in becoming what it is cannot be denied. Krit is
the last stronghold of monotheism (the belief in one all-power-
ful spiritual entity which controls the universe). The world is
known for supplying pilots for interstellar trade and shares
that distinction with Hobar. Followers of the Krit religion can
also be found on all the settled planets and especially on
Mora's World, where 90 per cent of the population actively
follows the tenets of the religion, and on Earth, where there
are more Krit co-religionists than on Krit itself (some sixteen
million in all).

Mora's World: Third planet of star G-98765. Colonized originally
four hundred years ago by miners but Krit colonists soon out-
numbered them. Mora's World is only six light-years from Krit,
and unmanned *sub* light speed ore cargo ships ply between
the two worlds. These are the only two stars where this is

possible economically. A similar situation exists between Lak and Hobar because these two planets share the same star. Mora's World is often considered to be a political satellite of Krit because they share the same theocracy (rule of religion) although the governments are considered separate for Confederation purposes.

CHAPTER EIGHT

STEPHEN LOCK

Each Krit of any importance was assigned a confidant.

Notorious conspiracies between Krit hierarchs and their confidants have been recorded in the history of the Krit theocracy. Even more notorious betrayals of Krits by their confidants have been recorded.

Yet the tradition prevailed.

The confidants have traditionally been monks of the Rose Order. The Rose Order was the only order of the twenty-seven orders which did not desex its monks. They were feared on Krit. Numerous overthrows of government for reasons of theology or reasons of power had been laid to that order.

At the time of the war, a member of the Rose Order was Chief Hierarch. He overthrew his predecessor, although he had not himself been his confidant. It was rumored that his predecessor's confidant had been in the pay of the current hierarch. Such rumors were softly whispered.

The Gray Order had a great control over commerce. Some pilots were of the Gray Order. Thus, the Gray Order was also powerful. They controlled the military for all practical purposes.

There was the problem of Stephen Lock. He had asked for a confidant in ignorance of the volatile situation, since he was not privy to the interplay of politics within the Krit system.

Though a brilliant politician in the Confederation structure, faith had made him blind to the possibility that a political structure might also exist on Krit.

The Rose Order was delighted. The Gray Order wanted to

retain their influence. A confidant, once asked for, was not to be denied. A small confrontation occurred behind the scenes. It was highlighted by two assassinations. Finally a compromise was reached.

Stephen Lock would have his confidant. He would be a man of learning with no political acumen. He would be a man of faith, exactly as Stephen Lock expected. He would be Philip of the House of Lazarus, a harmless dolt who happened to come from a very old house indeed. This was expected to please Faithful Stephen Lock and suited everyone else fine.

There was, however, a problem. What Philip lacked in political acumen, he more than made up for in theology and faith. As Professor Lin of Svid would often tell his students, every idea, every system of thought, contained the seeds of its own contradiction.

Krits, however, never thought in terms of ideas or systems of thought. They thought in terms of individuals. Ideas belonged to individuals. Destroy the individual and the idea went with him. This was a natural development for a people who saw the universe as the work of one individual.

So, whatever ideas Philip might implant in Stephen Lock could be purged by the removal of Philip if it came to that. Anyway, what was the harm in making Stephen Lock more of a believer? It was his belief that had driven him into the arms of the Krits in the first place.

What the Krit politicians didn't appreciate, or at least, what the politicians thrust to the back of their minds, was that a person either believed or didn't believe. There was no middle ground. A man like Philip could only refine Stephen Lock's belief.

What form would this refinement take? He would come to accept classical beliefs. Classical beliefs were somewhat in contrast to what was accepted generally as the Krit way.

After all, the original Krits were all true believers and they had spent many thousands of man-hours refining every aspect of the theology. The complexity of what emerged made the notions of modern psychologists seem like a child's mental exercise.

Krit indeed had two faces. One was the practical, everyday power—but always hovering in the background were the theologians. From these, every important heresy had emerged. Some of these heresies would have changed the face of Krit. One would have made war with the Confederation impossible. The heresy Stephen Lock would eventually lead would succeed so it would be called a reform. But that would happen after the war.

Krit had once been well thought of in the Confederation. It had been a haven for all those who protested the ambivalent modernism. It had been an outlet for the emotional man, the artist. It had been no great strain to blindly accept what Krit taught it one could work with one's hands.

Three hundred years before the war, a great architect had built the temple on Mora's World. He is nameless to history. He would have been shocked had he known what his adopted faith would lead to.

His great stone monument, enclosed in a transparent metal to protect it from Mora's violent atmosphere, now housed the headquarters of Stephen Lock's hordes. The great stone gallery he had placed over the temple had been used to plan the overthrow of all that that architect would have considered good.

Yet the architect would have laughed because the great building was very probably one of the factors that caused Stephen Lock's second important conversion. It was an overpowering place. Military headquarters or not, it brought peace to the mind of a sensitive person. It had been built with that purpose in mind.

Stephen Lock was a sensitive man.

It only remained for the place to clear itself of distractions. The generals and colonels had all left to meet the attack on Mora's World and Rainbow's End. All that remained was the planner of the defense, Stephen Lock, his confidant, Philip, and a stone statue of a naked man.

Every chart, all military machinery, radios and the like had gone with the generals and colonels. Security, in case that building fell into the hands of the Triangle, was given as the reason.

Stephen Lock was sitting on the ledge of a balcony overlooking a garden within the temple enclosure. "That young man in blue robes?"

"He belongs to the Order of Luke. They are teachers."

"There's a great deal I have to learn," Stephen said. He took a drink from the gold cup he had in his hand.

"Those are temporal concerns," Philip said. "They need not concern you."

Stephen nodded. "But I still have much to learn."

"I will teach you what little I know."

"Little?" Stephen asked angrily. "You sound like the Hobarians with their false modesty. Did they assign me a fool? Must I spill my soul to a fool?"

"No, General," Philip said smoothly, "it is a convention to speak with modesty. I am more than competent."

"Good. This politeness makes me suspect things that I don't want to know."

"That politics play a role in our affairs, Good Stephen?"

"Yes, exactly."

"It is the Contrary at work. I am not political. Neither are you. You are a general of the faith. I am a theologian of the faith. The politicians will go their way. We, or men like us, will remain. It is God's will."

"God has a thousand moods," Stephen repeated from scripture.

"God has one mood," Philip said with some nervousness.

Stephen turned toward him.

"You will have to learn Old English. Our modern tongue is a product of computerism . . . shortcut language." Philip was talking fast as if to get as much information in as possible. "The correct translation should be, 'God has one mood and he expresses it in a thousand ways.' But convention has made the other saying popular. Now, no one questions it. It's important that we men of responsibility understand exactly."

Stephen nodded. "You will teach me Old English." He walked across the gallery to the statue and stared at it. "What is this?"

"No one is sure. The builder brought it from Earth and no one tampers with what the builder has put in the temple. It is a most beautiful temple. God moved his hand."

"But a naked man?" Stephen asked. "Krits cover their bodies with modesty."

"No woman enters this place," Philip said, "and we know what a man is like."

"I know no man who looks like this. It looks like a heathen god. Did the builder make it?"

"No, General. It is much older. Tests have been run. It is older than the Krits. It was made before God gave my ancestor the *Book*. But no one knows about it."

"The model was a general like me," said Stephen.

". . . or a laborer who worked with his back," Philip interjected. "It is unlikely that a general stood still long enough for the craftsman to get his likeness. The builder of the temple called it 'David' and would say nothing more about it, according to the temple records."

"Umm. Well, general or laborer, I drink to you, statue. It seems as if this room was built around you. It is a pleasant room, don't you think so, Philip? It reminds me of Nice in many ways. There are many structures that look like this in Nice."

Philip kept his opinions to himself.

"I will confide in you, Philip. I am confused in matters of theology. Oh, I keep the Creed, but the Creed is a statement. . . . I don't know how to express it, Philip."

Philip was far from a dolt in understanding. "On Earth, Krit seemed different to you."

"Yes," Stephen nodded.

"The ways of men are the same all over. If you should go to Hobar, you will find them the same. It is only whether a person acts as God's agent or not. That's the only true test. God expresses Himself in a thousand ways."

"What does God want? No one has answered that except to say that God wants the Confederation defeated."

Philip was in a sweat. The critical moment had arrived.

Finally, Philip told him. "God wants followers. He wants men to know about Him. He has no other pleasure."

"Did God want this war?"

"The Council of Hierarchs wanted this war," Philip answered. "God was pleased with the state of things as they move at their pace." He half expected Stephen to strike him dead. But the truth was primary.

"What will I do?" Stephen asked, confused.

Philip, the theologian, now had more power than any Chief Hierarch had ever had in history. He could remake Krit in a true image of God's desire. He had no doubt that Stephen could take Krit. God had blessed Philip with the opportunity. Would the Contrary drain all his courage?

"You will continue with the war. Krit will lose it. Then you will take over as Chief Hierarch and set the children of God back on the path of righteousness."

"The Confederation will dissolve Krit."

"No," Philip said. "You still have power within the Confederation. You know how to avoid it. You know their way."

"Confidant, God intended for us to meet." He took another swallow of the wine and looked at the statue. "I know that emptiness now. Where are the artists that made statues like these . . . the sweating men . . . the scared boys that posed? Krit is not whole. I was kept from admitting it by the Contrary. You have the same politicians on Krit that I encountered on Earth. I will set the course straight. I swear it."

He threw his cup across the floor. It bent out of shape.

For Philip, it was the last night in this universe. He had not the courage to face the battle and jumped to his death from the top of the temple.

When the report of Philip's death came to Stephen, he assumed that God had called him once his life's mission was over. It was a confirmation.

A Keller transmission told him that Rainbow's End was still theirs.

His commanding pilot in orbit told him that the Triangle had met defeat at Mora's World too. They were repelled with heavy casualties.

His generals and colonels met to plan the attacks on Earth, Svid, and Hobar. His mind did not work on it much. His loyalties were now divided. He accepted the recommendations of his staff without comment. Had he not met Philip, Krit might have won decisive battles.

He let his mind work on the problem of overthrowing Krit

once the war was over. He began to guess instinctively whom he could count on for allies and who was doomed for the cross.

It was good that he held out on Mora's World and Rainbow's End. That would be a weapon in negotiating with the Confederation. He could blame the upcoming defeats on the Space Marshal who was thought responsible by the Krits.

By the time the evening wore on, he had forgotten Philip.

Interlude Eight: A Letter From Rass To A Lawyer on The Death of the Lawyer's Son

Rass
Technical Institute
Hobar
Nov. 19 (standard)
Dove 9 (local)

Hon. Miles M'Kur
Attorney-at-Law
37 Confederation Place
Suite 1198
Dakar, Senegal, EARTH

Honored Barrister:

Forgive this long delay in replying to your letter of August 11th (Keller Dot 665811). Unfortunately, I have war duties and they must be given priority even over the answer to a letter as important as your own.

You inquire as to the reason for the death of your son, Miles M'Kur, Jr., captain of Confederation standing. You say that you are not satisfied with the explanation given by the official Board of Inquiry, headed by myself, and that you expect a more rational answer. If one is not supplied you, you intend to press the Legislature (when it is reconstituted after the war) to hold formal hearings into the question of the unusually high death rate of pilots of Earth origin. You cite that three such pilots, including your son, have died in the last five years out of a total of twenty-seven.

There is little I can do except to make the Board of Inquiry's

findings a little less technical. If I could supply you with a
"reason" or "rational answer," be assured that I would. As to
your proposed hearing, I have informed Speaker Mahat's office
that I would like to see such a hearing convened and forwarded
your letter to the office with a request that you be called as a first
witness so that you can make the charges you stipulated in your
letter.

But frankly, sir, a legislative hearing will not solve the problem.
All they will be able to do is to confirm that all necessary pre-
cautions were taken on that fateful trip. The hearing will also
confirm that your son (and the other two fatalities) received the
best training. Indeed, your son graduated in the first 10 per cent
of his class—the first non-Hobarian to do so—and finished in the
usual time, being the second non-Hobarian to do that.

Master Avoy of the Albert School informed me that he fully
intended to make young Miles an assistant at his school in about
five years. Few Hobarians accomplish this in so short a time.

Furthermore, your son had completed twenty-five trips from
Earth to Svid and back. Another three trips and he would have
received his senior rating.

The Board of Inquiry could find no technical or human reason
why your son should have been lost. It therefore attributed it to
the physical effects of the vapor universe.

The reason for the high death rate of Earth pilots is, frankly,
coincidence. If you take any like period in the last one hundred
years, you will discover that there have been times when the
Krits have suffered high casualties and times when Hobar has
suffered high losses. Thirty years ago, the small world Grate lost
its only two pilots within the space of a month. For them, it was
a national tragedy. We have employed the best statisticians and
they can find no significant pattern that will help us reform our
curriculum to avoid these deaths. Experienced pilots and novices
are victims equally as often.

Your son would have been labeled an experienced pilot.

Your letter hints at institutional and technical failures when, in
fact, it is a failure of our ability to understand the nature of the
universe. We may have reached the point when our best intel-
lects cannot comprehend the forces that move the universe. As

you know, the transition element called the Ctz radical is not completely understood. We've never been able to put it under a microscope and we understand nothing of its nature except that a particular magnetic effect called the bottle, which is similar to gravity control, will capture it and release it at will. And even that is imperfect.

The bottle engines are built on the basis of experience rather than theory. There is no theory that holds. If an engine goes and a ship is lost, it is like the death of an individual. We cannot recover the engine to find out what went wrong. Nor can we call an individual back from death to find out what the "other world" is like.

I am not trying to be ironic but that is essentially the truth of the matter. The term "physical effects of the vapor universe" is a legal term to account for or categorize the loss of a ship for insurance purposes and record purposes and is not intended to explain "rationally" the loss of a ship in any scientific sense because without an over-all understanding of the Ctz radical, that is impossible.

The technology of the bottle has not changed radically since the original discoveries at the dawn of our Confederation and is not likely to until certain basic theories are formulated.

There is no "reason" why your son—or the 337 people he was carrying in suspended animation or the 800 pilots in the last six hundred years—were lost.

We can only continue with what we know or give up high-speed travel. In our profession, we can account for our failings only in the normal universe. In the vapor universe, we can only say, "due to the physical effects."

I mourn for your son and his passengers and for all the others who have passed from this universe. My mind fills with nightmares every time one of the pilots I trained is lost. If ever I thought I was responsible, I would resign my post.

Faithfully,
[signed] Rass

CHAPTER NINE

A ROYAL DEATH

"Damn it! Get after that thing."

Two ships immediately went scurrying after it. There would be little chance of catching it.

"Get on the Keller! Broadcast in the clear! I don't care. I don't want that bastard to reach Hobar's atmosphere."

"That's the second try in two days. Eventually they're going to get through. Better ask Commander Arin for further instructions. Use pinpoint if you have those new co-ordinates."

"Right, Captain."

"Can't reach him. He's all over the place. The Krits must have a hundred ships in the system."

"They're diversions, damn it. You'd better use the Keller. If one of those bacteriological weapons gets through . . ."

Mr. LaPorte was feeling uncomfortable. The atmosphere craft in which he was a passenger didn't have artificial gravity. He was strapped in. He could feel every bump and loop. It was a glider with a very small motor—something that would never fly on Earth but was all right for Hobar.

The pilot looked across to him and smiled.

The woman was enjoying his plight, Mr. LaPorte decided. He only hoped they would get to Ib Village soon. He felt his chest. The pack was still there.

He was going to meet the great Liennie.

There was ample evidence that the Krits still resented her and that any attempt at bacteriological warfare would be tried near her village. It had been evacuated of all but herself and a woman named Du. Liennie had insisted on evacuation. And she would not move, saying that if she did she would surely endanger a populated area. The Krits might get wind of it.

Mr. LaPorte, who felt responsible for Hobar's predicament, had done some insisting of his own. He would be at Ib Village, since it was the point of most danger. He felt he should be on hand to protect Liennie. He had acquired the most knowledge about bacteriological warfare, and his role in setting up emergency contingencies was now over.

It was a moral duty. The Hobarians had understood.

The woman who was piloting the glider touched the controls and the craft dipped. She pointed to some scattered buildings in a field of green.

That was Ib Village.

Mr. LaPorte nodded. He was beginning to feel airsick again but he held himself back. They would land soon.

He was left on the strip and the craft took off quickly. The pilot had war duties to return to. He quickly looked at a small map in his pocket and determined the location of the Ib School. It was a fifteen-minute walk.

He felt a little nervous as he knocked on the big wooden door. What would he say to such a person?

The door opened and a woman answered.

"Are you Mistress Liennie?" he asked.

"No, that's my mother. I'm Du. You must be Mr. LaPorte. Please come in. Mistress Liennie is in meditation. She will join us presently."

He was ushered into a large sunken room devoid of furniture except for a long low table in the center and some cushions.

"Have you word from Svid," Du asked, "and my husband, Captain Shear?"

"I've never been there. I don't think Svid has been attacked, though. We didn't receive any word on Keller transmission as of this morning."

Du nodded. "I will get you food." She left without waiting to see if Mr. LaPorte wanted any.

He tried to find a place to sit and felt awkward at the fact that no chairs were visible.

An older woman came in. She looked like she was in her forties but Mr. LaPorte knew she was approaching sixty (standard). She was dressed in a simple one-piece dress and had her head uncovered, unlike the younger Du.

"You're Mr. LaPorte of Earth," Liennie said.

He nodded.

Du walked in with a tray and put it on the table.

"Will you get Mr. LaPorte a chair, Du? He's not used to sitting on the floor."

Du left the room again and returned with a chair.

"Sit and be comfortable, sir," Liennie invited. She herself sat on the floor. "I have meats here and vegetables and some fruits. Eat. Would you like an alcoholic drink?"

"No thank you, ma'am." He pulled out his packet. "It's rather urgent that I explain these to you. The attack could come at any time. Will you have your daughter join us?"

Liennie bid Du to sit.

He spread the contents of the packet on the table. "Each of these kits contains six capsules. We think that we have all bacteriological agents covered with them. We were fortunate that your atmosphere precludes the use of more than a handful of the deadly germs. They are color-coded for each of half a dozen possible symptoms." He went on to describe the symptoms. "You must carry them with you at all times."

Liennie nodded and clipped her kit to the strap hanging around her waist. Du did the same. Mr. LaPorte already had his strapped.

"You must eat now," Liennie said, "and tell us what you've done for Hobar."

"I'm afraid that this whole thing was my fault." He went on to explain what had happened when he had been librarian on Earth.

Liennie already knew but let him speak. When he finished, she said, "I meant no offense by asking. I wanted to know about the preparations."

He nodded. "Every adult has one of these kits. We have

explained it to everyone. The children have been gathered in public buildings, and force fields have been activated around them. We hope that the fields will delay infiltration of the germs and that volunteers standing outside as well as machinery will give sufficient warning to properly inoculate each child. There are ships in orbit that we hope will serve as early-warning systems. You have telephones here?"

Liennie nodded just as the phone buzzed.

Mr. LaPorte's heart jumped while Du picked up the small receiver on the table. "It is Rass of the Institute wanting to know if you had arrived safely," Du said and told the caller that he had. She handed the phone to the librarian.

"Yes, sir. I have explained everything. . . . Yes, I will. . . . Good-by, sir." Mr. LaPorte put the receiver back on the table. "He sends you his regards, Mistress Liennie."

"He's a good man," she said. "Please eat, Mr. LaPorte."

He helped himself. "Aren't you going to eat?" he asked.

"I fast once a week. This is the day," Liennie said.

"May I ask why you refused to leave Hobar?" Mr. LaPorte asked.

"I cannot desert my station in times of stress. It is also likely that if I left, the Krits might attack a populated center. It is best that this disease strikes here first."

"You should have sent your daughter away," he said.

"She would not leave. None of my students could coerce her and I cannot fight my own daughter."

"I can't leave my mother," Du said simply.

"But I am here now. I know how to fight what's coming. Let me call a plane for you."

"No!" Du said. "I will stay with my mother."

Mr. LaPorte nodded. "If it doesn't cause you immodesty, Mistress, we should all sleep in the same room to aid each other when the time comes if it comes at night."

"There is no immodesty, sir. Will you tell me about Earth?"

Mr. LaPorte never had more attentive listeners. He spoke for several hours until he felt his throat parch. He apologized for talking about his job too much.

"You are so close to so much wisdom," Liennie said. "I can understand your dedication. Have you never married?"

He shook his head no. "I am small, I guess."

"The women of Earth are foolish," Liennie said, "to stay away from such a man as you, merely because you're small."

"And you, where is your husband?"

Liennie smiled. "We do not marry on Hobar as you understand it. We find men we like and live with them as long as it is mutually agreeable, though Du speaks of Peer Shear as her husband. She is of Krit and adopted by me. Our domestic relationships are kept simple. Now, of course, we have adopted some of the notions of other worlds and some marry."

"Who cares for the children?"

"No child is left uncared for. He may stay with his mother or father or another relative. Children decide that for themselves and often roam. Du's two girls are with an uncle they like very much. They come here for long stays very often."

"I guess that all those stories I hear are false."

Liennie smiled. "There is probably less immodesty here than on Earth as you understand immodesty. No, I best not say that. It is a prejudice."

"You're probably right, ma'am," Mr. LaPorte said with a smile.

Josephus Arin heard the good news first. It was the security ship flying a parallel course to his that had done it. They had intercepted one of the bacteriological weapons. The Hobarians were now pretty sure what they'd be facing.

"Security must not be relaxed. Emphasize that! This hell bomb will still take its toll," he ordered.

The captain of the security ship insisted on celebrating with a jury-rigged tea party. It was probably the first held on wide broadcast Keller since no one dared relax the vigil.

Josephus kissed the captain. "How fortunate that you're a woman," he said to general laughter, "but you'd better get back to your duties."

The long tedious wait resumed.

Liennie and Du entertained Mr. LaPorte with music that night. Liennie played a lively tune on her flute and Du played counterpoint on the yin-yang. The call from Rass telling them to have the blue capsule ready since that would probably counter the poison used had livened the evening.

The fact that Josephus' vigil had thus far prevented the contamination of Hobar did a great deal to bolster the spirits of Hobar. Still, Hobarians were under no illusion that an attack might not come.

"Why can't we just take the antidote now?" Du had asked.

"It's a poison in itself," Mr. LaPorte pointed out, "and dissipates quickly. That's the nature of the compound. Perhaps, if we had had more time . . ."

They had had very little time.

"Do you play anything, Mr. LaPorte?" Du asked.

"No," he said, embarrassed.

"A shame," she said. "When I was a Krit, I never knew music. Women weren't allowed to play anything. I am blessed to have met Liennie."

Mr. LaPorte could only nod and sit back and listen. The music was strange to him. It lacked drama and did not elevate like the sophisticated and complicated music of Earth. He would have called it primitive if he had known the terms used by experts. At first it seemed boring and he was tired. It became soothing and he fell asleep. It was a very light sleep from which he would wake every few minutes and realize where he was. He didn't want to be impolite.

Liennie and Du knew what was happening but continued playing. Tired people should sleep. They played more softly.

Mr. LaPorte was soon snoring.

The women laid out pillows and a blanket and helped him lie on the floor. They got their own bedding and slept within feet of him.

"They can't have too many more of these," Josephus said.

"They're cheap to make," a technician on his staff said. "That's eight we nailed."

"Well, what about the diversion?"

"Most of their ships are lost," a lieutenant said. "We're reforming."

"If I were a Krit commander, I'd hit now."

"You think they will?" the lieutenant asked.

Josephus nodded. "Before we can reform completely. I took a chance to block their bombs. I can't justify it militarily."

"Sir!" the lieutenant shouted. "Sixteen controls coming out at the sixth line."

"Where, damn it?"

"Arc 256 degrees, Plane 3 degrees."

It took a split second for it to sink in. "Their commander's an idiot," Josephus said. "He delivered his fleet right to our door. What can I say? Get them!"

The lieutenant smiled. "Right, sir!"

"The man must be a blundering fool," Josephus mumbled. "Emerging only six million miles from Lak. He'll never detach his pods in time. What in the Krit hell is going on?" He looked over the lieutenant's shoulder to confirm it. He was talking to himself with delight. "They couldn't possibly have sent that as a diversion. It's too large . . . no reason." He remembered that he'd been a spy. "Maybe we have a friend on Krit." Turning to the lieutenant, he said. "You just keep the Third Squadron near Hobar! We won't need them."

He continued mumbling. "All that planning . . . all that allocation for this purpose and that . . . and their commander turns out to be an idiot. They'll never touch us." He couldn't believe it. It couldn't possibly be a trick.

He turned to the lieutenant again. "Are those pods dummies?"

"No, sir. It's the invasion army intended for Lak. No way to fool these instruments. They're the same we use to check passengers in suspended animation in the vapor universe. They're foolproof in normal space. Roughly a hundred thousand soldiers, I'd guess."

"They're dead," Josephus concluded. "Their commander's an idiot. In six minutes, they're dead. Get a fusion bomb dead center!" he ordered needlessly.

"It's on its way," the lieutenant said.

Mr. LaPorte woke up choking. Heavily he rose from the floor. His pants were still on. It took him a few seconds to adjust his thinking but a bacteriological bomb had obviously hit. He broke open the capsule with the blue markings and pressed it against his thigh. Where are the women, he thought in a panic. His eyes adjusted to the dark. He saw the two figures on the floor and ran to the one who was also choking. He didn't know which it was. He broke open her capsule and pressed it against her thigh.

He went to the other. She was still. He broke open her capsule and repeated the operation. He knew in his heart that it was too late.

He fumbled for a light switch and finally found it.

It was Liennie and she was dead.

An empty feeling overcame him and he struggled to the spot Du was lying on and shook her.

She opened her eyes slowly, heavily.

"Your mother is dead," he said slowly, his throat still choking.

Du was in a state of shock. She didn't understand.

He went to the telephone and dialed the Institute. "Rass . . . where is he? All right. . . . Yes. . . . I'll do the best I can . . . a transport in the morning . . . hands full . . . few deaths . . . force field was no good. . . . Yes, I understand completely. . . . Yes, Liennie is dead. . . . She wouldn't want that. . . . Take care of the living." He hung up.

When he turned from the telephone, he saw Du leaning over her mother. "She's been dead for hours," she told Mr. LaPorte. Softly, she continued, "Why her? She was the strongest of us all."

Mr. LaPorte went to Du. "I'm sorry."

Du said nothing. She did not even cry but sat on her heels over the body.

The transport came the next morning. Rass was on it.

"I failed you," Mr. LaPorte said.

Rass looked at him. "You saved her daughter. There's no point in attaching blame to yourself."

"How many were lost?" Mr. LaPorte asked.

"Forty thousand," Rass answered. "Look, Mr. LaPorte. We were lucky. It could have been half the population. You feel guilty and the squadron that missed those three bombs also feels guilty. Go on with life, sir. We're going to need people like you to rebuild. If you insist on atonement, stay on Hobar and work for the public good."

Rass walked off with the mourners' party.

Du came over to him and took him by the arm. She led him to the transport. She whispered to him, "I accept my mother's death. It saved countless others who might have been the target for the bomb that exploded a dozen miles from here. If you insist on guilt, you do her death no honor. You must accept it without guilt. Guilt is a function of pride. . . . Be humble!"

Interlude Nine: Preface to The Soldier's Guide
(Thought to have been written by
Jewette Lin)

Every society has had conventions, laws, and regulations concerning whom it was proper for the individual to kill and not to kill. These rarely need formal elucidation. Every citizen of that society knows it inwardly and has enough moral sense to discriminate borderline situations. The individual rarely makes an error which calls for a review by one of society's institutions (such as a court of law).

We are now faced with war, which is new to our society.

The Confederation War Council thus sets the following guidelines which will forthwith be considered as a legal "defense" should questions ever arise:

1. Any armed enemy of the Confederation, declared or undeclared. An armed enemy shall be considered any individual or group of individuals which poses a direct threat to any citizen or group of citizens belonging to the Confederation. (Thus a weaponless Krit threatening one or more Confederation citizens shall be considered armed. A Krit using as a weapon a device or instrument normally used for peaceful purposes shall be considered armed.)
2. Any enemy of the Confederation who might reasonably pose a threat if left alive.
3. Any Allorg android.
4. Any collaborator who by some action or statement of intent threatens any Confederation citizen.

If a Krit wishes to surrender and in some way shows his good intent he should be allowed to do so. No Allorg android falls into this classification. They are not intelligent and will be destroyed as soon as possible. When in doubt, kill.

CHAPTER TEN

SVID UNDER SIEGE

Dr. Margaret Moore was near hysterics. "You don't care, do you?"

"No," admitted Arlin Elvuse.

"You disgrace that uniform," she concluded.

"The uniform does not make the man. The man makes the uniform." It was a stupid thing for him to say and he knew it.

She stormed out of his office.

Arlin looked around at the walls. He was in charge of propaganda. No staff had been spared him. He was alone. He had fallen to spit and polish for lack of something to do. It was a popular war. They didn't need a propaganda officer. When someone is not needed, he is generally promoted.

Arlin Elvuse was now a colonel. On his collar was the insignia he himself had designed. As far as he knew, no one else in Svid's army was a colonel. They were sergeants and lieutenants and majors and commanders. Captains were pilots. He was the only colonel.

He made an appearance now and then and was well liked as an entertainer, but that eventful time when serious preparations were needed had come. No one had time for Arlin Elvuse.

But Dr. Moore had made his day. She had proved that passions were aroused in war. He had looked forward to it with a kind of dread. Now he saw what it was like. The dread was gone.

Dr. Moore had come to him to appeal to his friend, Commander Lin, for another expedition to try to rescue the natural

Allorgs. "They are the germ of a new civilization," she had told him.

"Like this one?" he had asked flippantly.

And she had blown up. Dedication scared him. He despised it with a passion he hid behind his personal charm. He envied it, he knew. Just the ability to sit and solve a complex problem that took years to even formulate made him envious. These bright youngsters who could grasp a basic science when he could barely understand an algebraic equation made him envious.

It never occurred to Arlin Elvuse that these same bright young people envied him for something they could not grasp—an understanding of men. They would formulate complex problems about human relationships in mathematical terms because that's all they understood, and then they would be rendered shy by the first boisterous individual that came along.

It was a mutual envy but Arlin Elvuse, the former Clown, could never grasp this.

He let this lack of understanding explain why he didn't care for the Allorgs. They seemed part of the scientific world, not his. He resented the scientist's ally. He had never met an Allorg.

Arlin had often told himself that he was no longer capable of passion when he really was afraid of it. Professor Lin had conquered passion while Arlin had merely put it aside.

He left his office. As soon as the door closed, the noise of the hallway filled with busy men dawned on him. Standing across from him was a Hobarian pilot. He was leaning against a wall.

Arlin looked at him and the pilot sensed it. He turned and smiled.

For some irrational reason, Arlin walked over to him. "It's a long wait, isn't it?"

"They'll come soon enough," the brawny pilot said.

"Second squadron?" Arlin asked. Another stupid question. A large patch marked "Two" was sewn to the man's coveralls.

"Yes. I don't recognize your uniform?"

"Arlin Elvuse. Propaganda office. I'm a colonel."

"Oh, you're the people that put out all the manuals," the pilot said.

Arlin nodded and smiled. It was true. His office—that is, he—

had put out all the manuals. It was good to be reminded that he had done some useful things.

"Now I remember," said the pilot. "You're the person that put all those funny things in them to get everyone to read the manuals. It was a good idea."

Arlin felt much better.

"I have to go now," Arlin said and waved to the man.

He intercepted a clerk and asked which way it was to Dr. Moore's office. He was directed to the right corridor. Finding the door, he knocked.

Dr. Moore herself answered. She was alone in the room.

"I came to apologize, Doctor," he said, letting himself in. "I will speak to Jewette for you. You're right. I'm sorry." He was lying since he had been at the conference when the matter had been discussed at length and rejected as impractical. But his job was to give comfort, he decided.

She closed the door. "I'm sorry for all this mess." There were books all over the floor.

"It only shows that you're working," Arlin said. "My office is clean, which shows you how much work I do."

She let a smile grow on her face.

"What are you supposed to do when the attack comes?"

She fumbled around in her pocket and pulled out a small energy weapon. "They told me to stay out of the way when they issued me this." She was pointing it at him.

He pushed her hand aside. "I hope they showed you how to use it."

He pulled out his. It was the same model. "They probably don't think the Allorgs will land or they wouldn't have trusted me with one of these," he said deadpan.

He had her in a wide smile.

"When will you speak to Commander Lin?"

He rubbed his chin. "As soon as the battle is fought. I don't think he wants to be bothered now. You have to be careful in choosing the proper time." He changed the subject. "Come to lunch with me. It's nearly time."

They walked across the campus of Oberland University to a temporary building put up as a mess hall. Svids generally ate alone or with family or friends. The institution of public dining had never really made an impact. But war requires efficiency and easily puts aside minor notions of propriety. The mess hall was built and was always crowded.

The Hobarians had insisted on making no distinction between enlisted or drafted personnel and officers as had been the tradition in the police forces of Svid. They had felt that since most Hobarians were, of necessity, officers, this might cause bad feelings. They had found support from Arlin, who had been consulted.

It was one of the functions given to the former Clown to review all organizational plans. This had been done at the insistence of Commander Lin who thought that some undesirable institutions or practices might develop from the war and that Arlin was the best man to spot them at conception.

Arlin was well chosen for the task. The officer corps had no other function but to lead in their own specialty. They had no privileges and were not given special respect. The word "sir" was reserved for those a person respected. This was all Arlin's doing. He had given many hours to studying ancient armies, probing for their weak and strong points.

The organizational chart of the Triangle Force read like a parallel of the civilian organization prior to the war. Men were truly leaders in peace and war.

Of course, no one anticipated a standing army after the war and even Arlin realized that it was only during peacetime that obnoxious practices developed. No one had time during the war. Arlin anticipated being on hand after the war to "demoralize" any attempt at these practices.

So it was that Arlin Elvuse and Dr. Margaret Moore found it difficult to find a place to sit. The place was crowded. Finally they sat between two enlisted men. Their plastic trays were tightly squeezed between the two others, which in turn were tightly squeezed all along the long table.

"The food has gotten more basic since the war," Arlin said. "I thought I'd be the first casualty but it turned out that the first casualty was the culinary arts."

"It's got everything you need to live," the biologist said. "I had a hand in preparing it. It's probably the first time Svid has had a balanced diet on a nationwide level."

"No offense meant, Doctor," Arlin quipped, "but you're a bad cook."

"I'll see that cooking is added to the university curriculum after the war," she said.

"I hope I last . . ."

A siren in the distance interrupted him. All 657 persons in the mess hall fell silent.

They heard the siren again. It was a clear tone which seemed far away.

A man, whom Dr. Moore recognized as Commander Rone, stood up. "Don't be alarmed," he said to the gathering. "Sit quietly."

All eyes were on him as he spoke quietly into his personal telephone. He put the instrument away and said to the group, "All backup pilots to your ships! The Krits have appeared at the seventh line. There's a battle in progress. Ground forces personnel, finish your lunch and report back to your units immediately afterward!"

A mixed company of Hobarians and former Svid shuttle pilots, peppered with more recently trained men, rose as one and began leaving.

Someone started clapping and the personnel in the mess hall burst into applause for the fifty or so men as they quickly walked out, led by Commander Rone. The Commander turned briefly and saluted the men and women in the room in the Hobarian manner, the right fist in the left hand. He bowed slightly and left.

"What do we do now?" Dr. Moore asked.

"Why don't we go to my office and tune in on the news?"

She nodded.

Everybody was rushing as they left the temporary building, going to assigned stations or specified shelters.

Once the door was closed, Arlin's office was silent. He went to his telephone and placed it on the general channel only to hear that it was going off the air so that it could not be used as a navigation device.

Arlin had known all along that it would go off the air, but for a reason he hadn't verbalized to himself, he thought Dr. Moore should remain with him.

Someone knocked at the door. He opened it.

It was a young student Dr. Moore recognized but didn't know personally. "Everyone has been ordered to leave the university area," the young woman told them. "It's likely to be bombed."

"Bombed?" Dr. Moore said in disbelief. "The Library . . . the laboratories. Arlin, can we do something?"

"Not if they plan to bomb it!"

"They wouldn't destroy a university," Dr. Moore said, shocked.

"They were willing to destroy a race," Arlin reminded her.

"No." She shook her head in disbelief. "They'll try to capture the university. They need it."

Arlin breathed a long sigh. "I doubt that they think as you do."

But Dr. Moore was not about to give up the university. "We must stay. Whole lives' works are here."

Arlin thought that it was illogical but he liked the bravado displayed by the diminutive lady biologist. He was perfectly willing to stay with her, no matter how militarily irrational she was. "It's a chance but I suppose it won't hurt us to have some kind of defense setup."

"Are there any soldiers around?" Dr. Moore asked.

"Everyone has been ordered to leave the university area," the student repeated.

"I can't order anyone to stay with us," Arlin told Dr. Moore. "It's very likely that they'll bomb the place."

The student spoke up. "I'll stay with you." She pulled her personal telephone from her pocket and called her fellow students to come to Room 1640, Arlin's office.

"I won't allow it," Dr. Moore said when she saw the six assembled students. "None of you are over fifteen."

"I agree. You're all much too young," Arlin said. "Get to your designated shelter areas."

"It's our university, too," the girl said. "We have a right."

"No you don't," Arlin said.

"Then we'll form our own defense squad."

"The hell you will," Arlin said. "You don't even have guns."

"There's a whole supply room full of chemicals and we can make fire bombs. Gerald has a junior chemist's rating."

"I could never explain it to your parents," Dr. Moore told them.

"We're not asking you to," Gerald said.

Arlin was thoughtful. "If they were going to play with chemicals, we'd accept it and give them proper supervision."

Dr. Moore was still against the whole idea.

"You'll have to obey my orders," Arlin told them. "I'm an officer and you're all privates."

They all nodded.

"It's going to be a damn children's crusade. . . ."

"What?" Dr. Moore said.

"Never mind—history. We'll just make sure the Italians don't sell the children into slavery this time."

Dr. Moore wore a blank expression.

Outside the compound they ran into a sergeant.

"Nevin Baze!" Dr. Moore said in surprise.

"I've come to pick up stragglers. There's a truck on the other side of the mess hall."

"Your orders have just been canceled. We're staying," Arlin said, "and I need you to supervise these young criminals."

"What?" Baze said.

"Never mind," Arlin said. "Get your truck out of sight and meet us in the Chemistry Block. You know where it is?"

Baze nodded and ran off.

"You know him?" Arlin asked.

"Oh yes. He's very brave. He saved my life on Allorg. They promoted him when we returned."

"Good, I can use an experienced noncom," Arlin said and he led the party to the Chemistry Block. Arlin had to punch a hole in the door with his energy weapon to break the lock. "I hope one of you knows where everything is."

Dr. Moore apparently did. She started giving directions to the students and started punching buttons on the lab machinery. "I think one-ounce bottles will do to stop an Allorg. They'll be easy to throw."

"Make them two-ounce," Arlin said. "Some weight is needed to travel against the wind."

"Two ounces it is," Dr. Moore agreed.

"What are you putting in them?"

"Something simple and effective—hydrochloric acid. Destroys tissue on contact and is painful. It will create shock even in mindless androids."

"Make something that'll burn on shattering, too," Arlin said, "and dye it a different color."

She nodded.

Within ten minutes the lab machinery had enough for everyone to carry.

She told the assembled gathering, "These are Number Six containers. You can drop them and they won't shatter but if you throw them a few yards, they will. It's all standard laboratory fare."

Baze returned. "I had a rifle in the truck. Does anyone know how to use one?"

The girl who had first contacted them said that her brother had shown her how. She had done target shooting.

Baze gave her the rifle and took some bottles, which he was told how to use.

"Now, what do we protect?" Arlin asked. "It's your show, Doctor."

"The library. We can seal off the side entrances with furniture and force them to come through the front."

Arlin nodded. The library had been built ten years before and had been duly dubbed Frazer's Folly because of the architect's complex, almost Byzantine design. He had made a number of uncomplimentary comments about it at the time, but its very complexity might save their lives. He made a mental note to send a letter of apology to Frazer, though he expected to forget it. He'd make a point of forgetting. It was still poor architecture.

The preparations were swift. All the students knew the premises well and it was easy. Eventually the waiting came.

Arlin did make contact with the army by phone. The officer

he spoke to told him that the university was sure to be bombed and that he and his party should evacuate at once.

Arlin repeated the officer's recommendation and added that for himself, he agreed with the analysis.

Dr. Moore would not be moved and Arlin shrugged his shoulders.

It turned out that the Krits did not want to bomb the university until a party they planned to send to capture it had found documentary evidence that the heretic, Alanis, was indeed dead and that Professor Lin had written the heretic *Book* instead. They had been having trouble with the heretic text at home. Professor Lin was a good forger.

The Krits did not know that the evidence they sought was not at the university but at Lin's home. They thought it was in the library. After finding the evidence, they would bomb the university and all its pagan works.

As fate would have it, Dr. Moore's little party, if they could hold out, would save the university from bombing. She was only wrong about why.

Arlin and the military thinkers were right that the Krits had no use for the university. They just didn't have all the facts about the *Book*.

Nine individuals might just save the intellectual life of a planet from damage that would take generations to repair.

There was also the possibility, which Arlin hoped for since he believed a fusion bomb would fall in the area, that Commander Lin's forces would prevent any Krit from breathing Svid's atmosphere. Having attended numerous war councils, Arlin knew that to be a remote possibility.

The Triangle Force would move in on the invasion fleet from two points, like a pincer. One would be under Peer Shear and the other would be under Commander Rone after an initial battle by another wing had slowed the Krit advance. Arlin looked at his timepiece. The alert wing in space would have retreated by this time and fallen back to join the two pincer squadrons. The battle would be in progress.

It was a classic strategy devised by Professor Lin and it would work given the consideration that the Krits would not commit their entire fleet to the operation. That, they would save for Earth.

Still, a great many landing crafts would get through.

"How long?" asked Baze.

"It won't be for several hours yet," Arlin said. "See if you can get the kids to sleep a little. Give them some sleeping tablets. Here, I have some in my pocket."

"You have trouble sleeping," Dr. Moore said.

"Standard officer's equipment," replied Arlin.

Arlin's personal telephone buzzed. He pulled it out of his pocket and turned the volume up. "Elvuse here."

"This is Altaire. What are you doing?"

"Defending man's right to learn the complexity of his ignorance."

"I've received word that you are at the university. Take your people out of there. They'll be killed."

Arlin turned to Dr. Moore. She was resolved.

"Sorry, old friend, but a charming little lady has a date with some Allorgs here."

"Are you insane, Arlin? You know they're going to fusion-bomb the place. Look, at least sixteen of their ships have gotten through thus far. I can guarantee that they'll walk right through our orbital defense. That's our weakest line. We've already dispersed the population from the cities."

"Thanks for the tip." He turned from the phone and announced, "We will definitely have visitors."

"Arlin," Altaire said, "this is a direct order. Get out! If any of those people die, you will be charged with murder and I'll be the prosecutor."

"I don't deserve such attention from so great a barrister," Arlin said. "If they fusion-bomb the place, you'll have to try me in the Krit hell, and if they attack with conventional forces, then I'm justified in defending the library."

A few seconds elapsed before Altaire spoke again. "You son of a bitch! You should have been a lawyer. Do one thing for me. Let any of your people go if they want to."

"They're all volunteers except Sergeant Baze."

"I'm a volunteer now, sir," the youth said, overhearing the former Clown.

"Ask them all again," Altaire said and hung up.

Arlin turned and told Baze to get everyone over to his position. They all wanted to stay. Arlin couldn't paint the picture black enough for them to leave. He ordered them all to get some sleep and had Baze pass out the sleeping pills. "You too, Dr. Moore."

She obeyed.

Three hours later he was called again by Altaire and told that he had less than a half hour (standard).

Arlin looked at his watch and shook Baze awake. He gave him the antidotes for the pills and ordered everyone awake.

Arlin was the first to hear the rumble of a shuttle as it approached for a landing. "Damn if you weren't right, Dr. Moore. They're landing." He looked at his timepiece. "And a few minutes early to boot. It's not like the Krits to take an interest in the sciences. I wonder what they're up to."

"They may need to steal some research materials," she offered.

"What, for instance?" Arlin asked.

Dr. Moore couldn't think of anything specific.

"All right, everybody. Take your positions." He went to a window to see the craft land. It was dark outside and the craft had brazenly left on its running lights. The thing went silent just before it landed. It had expensive antigravity devices. They were definitely after something.

"Do you think they'll come here?" Baze asked.

"Ask Dr. Moore. She's been calling the cards as they've fallen," Arlin replied.

Arlin watched thirty of the giant Allorgs emerge from the ships followed by three Krit officers. He called the military dispatcher and was told that at least six divisions had landed in the area. They'd have to do the best they could alone.

Arlin went to Dr. Moore's side. "They're marching three abreast as if they planned no fighting and only one ship. There must have been a spy in the headquarters to tell them that no defense had been planned for the university."

"So it wasn't the bombing that you were afraid of. You just didn't want to bother saving the university," she accused.

"You're wrong, Doctor. We thought we'd minimize the danger to the university by leaving it free of defenders. It's an old trick many nations have used in ancient times to preserve art treasures. We still thought the Krits might bomb it. We just did what seemed reasonable. They have no respect for our kind of 'treasures.' We let it slip that no one would be here. That's also an old trick in case there was a spy and I guess there was. No time for talk now. Listen carefully," he addressed the group. "We have a tactical advantage if we pull back to those balconies up there and let them march in. When they're all in and boxed up, we let them have it."

"Let them in the library?" said Dr. Moore, shocked.

"In the lobby, Doctor," Arlin corrected. "All that is here are a few extremely ugly sculptures of dubious worth. We'll be doing the art world a favor. What has to be saved is behind those doors we welded a few hours ago."

Baze said, "The sculptures look valuable."

"I'm sure the sculptor will forgive us," Arlin said. "Move and don't fire until I do. You with the rifle, stand up there and pick off the Krit officers bringing up the rear. That's your only job, understand? We'll get the androids."

The girl nodded and climbed the elaborate steps.

There were no lights in the lobby and it was one of those modern buildings without windows. The defenders would have the advantage. Arlin made another mental note to have Frazer design a fortress for him if he ever needed one.

There were a few seconds of silence and the outer doors burst into a hundred pieces from an energy weapon.

Now, if only those kids don't panic, thought Arlin.

Light poured in from the outside but the balconies were out of range of the beams. "Thank you, Frazer," Arlin whispered.

The thirty androids marched in three abreast followed by the Krits with their lights.

Before they could move them up the stairs, Arlin threw a bottle of liquid fire into the android ranks. Soon the floor below was ablaze. A man screamed. A Krit had apparently been hit with hydrochloric acid. Allorg androids had no vocal chords according to a briefing he'd attended.

The automatic fire-fighting equipment came into play.

Arlin hadn't counted on that. The chemicals were so thick that they neutralized the fire bombs on contact. "Baze, get everybody out of here. I can handle the rest."

Five of the Allorgs were still alive.

"Go! Get out of here!"

Baze led the students out the back, the girl protesting that she hadn't had a chance to fire her rifle.

"You too, Dr. Moore, out!"

"I stay," she said emphatically.

The five androids spread out under the fire of the energy weapons. One fell. Two. Three. The other two had reached cover and were firing back.

"They've made them semi-intelligent," Dr. Moore said as they both ran for cover.

The androids were soon up on the balcony. Semi-intelligent was right. They had exhausted their weapons on more of Frazer's work.

"They can't see very well," Dr. Moore explained.

"I rather think they're the art critics of our time. Where's your gun?"

"I dropped it."

"Mine's out. Where did you drop it?"

"I don't know."

The androids turned. There was nothing wrong with their hearing.

Arlin looked for an exit but the androids were between them and the only exit, the stairs. All there was was an elaborate sculpture consisting of a sphere made up of hard alloy rods converging at the bottom and top. Inside the sphere was a flat triangular piece. "Get in!" he told Dr. Moore. She had no trouble squeezing through the rods. He had to take his jacket off. The bars were absolutely rigid.

They sat in the center of the twenty-foot-diameter sphere on the triangle. There was no possibility of the androids reaching them or bending the bars and they weren't intelligent enough to go down to the lobby and get one of the fallen energy weapons. The androids stood outside reaching in but they didn't have enough arm length.

"What do they call this thing we're in?" Arlin asked.

"'Algebraic prison.' There's a sign over there."

"That figures," Arlin said. "See if you can lie down and get some sleep. I'll keep watch. Baze will be back soon with reinforcements."

"Do you have any more of your pills?"

He looked in his pocket. "I left them in the jacket." The jacket was lying outside the cage. "Shall I get it?"

"No," she said. "Don't joke like that."

Arlin watched for some hours while Dr. Moore fell asleep on his shoulder. He woke her up at just past midnight. "What's wrong with them?"

She looked at the two androids which were now down on their knees. She had to think for a few seconds. "They're starving. A biological machine constructed as simply as they wouldn't have a terribly sophisticated digestive system. It wouldn't store food for long."

"How long before they're dead?"

"What time is it?"

"Midnight plus twenty minutes (standard)."

"They won't last another hour," she said, "given their mass and probable last feeding time."

So they waited an hour and fifteen minutes more until both of the androids were on the floor.

"You're sure it's not a trick?" Arlin asked.

"They could have gone to the lobby and picked up a gun."

"Right, it was just a nervous question."

They eased themselves out of the sphere. She was about to bend over and check one of the androids but he stopped her. "He may still have enough strength to pull you apart."

Arlin led Dr. Moore down to the lobby where he picked up one of the energy rifles that still looked usable. He peeked out the door. Nothing. The ship, its running lights still on, stood silently. "I'm going to investigate. You stay here and mind the books."

Using the cover of the dark as much as possible, he reached

the ship. The door was wide open. He entered to no other danger than the harsh smell of the interior, which he took to be the smell of the Allorgs.

In the control room he found two hairless individuals, both quite old, cringing in fear.

"Who are you?" Arlin asked.

"Monks," one said quickly. "We came to see about the *Book*."

"Book? What book?"

He couldn't make sense of the explanation they gave him. They were too scared to make any sense. He took out his telephone and called the military dispatcher. "I've got a couple of prisoners for you at the university."

"You and everybody else," the dispatcher answered.

"We won?" he asked.

"I'm not a Krit dispatcher, am I?" the man at the other end replied. "We wiped the slate clean. The only thing we can't figure is why they tried a landing without first winning the space battle."

"This is Arlin Elvuse, dispatcher. Can you contact me with Altaire?"

"I'll try."

It took the man a few seconds.

"Arlin, it's good to hear your voice. How did it go?"

"We held the library. Dr. Moore turned out to be right."

"Really? Well, I still think you were lucky. We got hit by half a dozen fusion bombs. A couple of them hit the outskirts of Oberland. Stay in buildings. We're not sure about radiation levels yet. Didn't you feel them?"

"We were pretty busy and we're pretty far out of the city. Listen, I've got a couple of prisoners—Krit monks. They're talking about some book or other."

"We'll let Professor Lin interrogate them when he gets a chance. He'll enjoy that. Is Dr. Moore all right?"

"Yes. Did my squad get back safely?"

"I don't know. We have a lot of displaced people."

"Well, I chased them out of the area at around nineteen hundred (standard). I assumed they'd be coming your way."

"We had things pretty wrapped up by then. They'll probably turn up. Will I have to prosecute you?"

"Not unless the squad disappears between here and where you are."

"Glad to hear it. Why don't you join me for dinner tomorrow? We can talk then. It looked as though this Stephen Lock isn't the military commander we thought. I could have caused us more damage and I know nothing of strategy."

"Maybe he had a change of heart," Arlin said and closed the circuit.

Interlude Ten: Two News Stories
From The SVID TRANSFAX
(Front page and interstellar edition)

Oberland—It was announced Wednesday by the government press office that Altaire, a prominent Svid attorney and diplomat, has been named referee of the War Insurance Act.

In a simple announcement, the Board of Selectmen of the City of Oberland called the lawyer "one of the most outstanding citizens in the municipality. He is trusted and well liked and is more than qualified."

(The next paragraph was inserted in the interstellar edition only.)

On the planet Svid, the Board of Selectmen of the City of Oberland is the world government. Selectmen are elected from all municipalities in the Svid nation. This tradition goes back to the beginning of colonization. The City of Oberland and other municipalities are run by what are called Second Councils on predominantly urban Svid. Another tradition is to speak of Svid as a municipality in formal government announcements.

Reached the same afternoon, Altaire explained the new legislation:

"First, it puts a moratorium on all insurance payments for the duration of the war and three standard months afterward. This is to prevent widespread bankruptcies which would make it impossible for anyone to collect insurance on war damages.

"The government will take over the operation of all insurance companies and pay all claims as if they were government debts. These payments will be based on existing policies. Since over 99 per cent of Svid lives and properties are insured, we thought that this was the best way to handle the situation. Those without insurance may apply for relief which will be paid at the discretion of my staff. At the end of a year after the war, totals will be tabulated and will be considered loans to the companies to be repaid at no interest over a forty-year period or at 2½ per cent a year. During the same period, insurance rates will rise 2½ per cent. Thus we will be spreading our debt over a forty-year period.

"Since Svid controls 67 per cent of all insurance business in the Confederation, this service will be extended to off-world policy holders. We will, upon request, also take over insurance companies owned by non-Svid interests and apply the same formula. This will be done at the discretion of my staff and will depend on the active supportive legislation of the governments concerned.

"In effect, we are using the industrial standing of Svid to back the whole society. We anticipate a slight inflation, but no one will notice since salaries and property values will increase correspondingly. Pensions will also be adjusted by this Act.

"Some will ask where the real losses will be felt. They won't be. Accelerated growth which is being planned will cover them nicely."

Altaire went on to say that co-operation was expected from all quarters. A number of off-world insurance companies had already approached his office.

Asked about the controversial provision which will make it possible for former enemies to take part in the plan, he said that rebuilding has no enemies. He hopes that public passion will not make it impossible to enforce this provision. "After all, Svid has built its reputation on fair dealing and many Krit corporations and individuals are insured by Svid concerns. The war does not cancel these contracts unless the Krit government dissolves the contracts by some action. It would not be sound policy on their part since it would affect their credit and they aren't industrially self-sufficient."

"It is my hope that all combatants will eventually look upon this war as a temporary madness and that the Confederation will again stand united and all the stronger for this mistake. The implementation of the provision cannot happen without the active co-operation of Krit."

Altaire pointed out that while the government would direct the insurance companies, they planned on using existing personnel and staff. The direction, he explained, will be in the form of additionally needed personnel and regulations.

- 30 -

Page six of the entertainment section
(local edition only)

Oberland—the architect and sculptor J. S. Frazer announced a civil lawsuit against Arlin Elvuse for dafamation of character by action.

He accused the former Svid Clown of deliberately luring a Krit party into the library at Oberland University and using the attack as an excuse to destroy what Frazer called his "immortal works."

Frazer said that the Clown had always been against him and that he (Frazer) had never acted against him because the status of Clowns was traditionally considered to be immune to lawsuits of this type. "Arlin has resigned, however," Frazer said, "and can no longer hide behind that ridiculous costume for this obvious case of slander to my immortal works."

A number of prominent lawyers consulted by the *Transfax* said that the suit would be thrown out of court and suggested that it was a publicity stunt by an artist of questionable reputation. The lawyers asked not to be named. "I *can* be sued," one of them said. "I can't afford to waste the time defending myself, though I'd probably win," he pointed out. They also questioned the legal right of a Clown to resign since the post has only quasi-legal standing.

Arlin Elvuse was reached by telephone. He said, "I usually wait until an artist is dead before I call his works immortal."

- 30 -

CHAPTER ELEVEN

THE DIVINE HORDE

Peer Shear's office on Svid contained Professor Lin, Arlin Elvuse, Margaret Moore, and Peer Shear.

"Lock will be assembling the remains of his fleet plus reinforcements from Allorg," Shear said. "Intelligence has it that they've abandoned production of the androids. I think it's going to be a make-or-break situation with the attack on Earth. I've had communications from Josephus Arin and he agrees that the key battle will be Earth but Keller transmission is wide open and our code could feasibly be cracked so I didn't dare consult further. Now is the time for speculation. Where will they assemble? What will they have to attack with?"

Dr. Moore spoke first. "They may have as many as two million androids left."

"They can't transport them all," Elvuse said. "I went over the books with the shipyards here. They haven't the controls or the pods to do it and it's inconceivable that they got to build more than a few hundred pods. They never had the facilities to build controls. The people I spoke to at your request, Peer, thought that in any drawn-out conflict, they'd lose because of their lack of a real industrial base."

Shear nodded. "It explains the make-or-break situation. How many could they transport?"

Elvuse said, "This is the best guess of the engineers at the yards. Assuming they use all controls at their disposal and protect their home planet and holdings only with interplanetary craft, they could transport a half million Allorgs and that's assuming they had no fighter crafts to transport. They'll have to have fighter crafts of course so it'll be much less."

"I'd guess they'd bring a minimum of fighters," Professor Lin said. "They see Earth as basically a ground-combat situation, as we do."

"How could they do that?" Shear asked. "Mahat has the Earth defenses as tight as could be imagined."

"Suppose that they assembled elsewhere and came in under already existing battle orders?" Professor Lin asked.

"Yes," Shear said, "that's exactly how I'd do it if I wanted to take a planet with the population Earth has. The question is where will they assemble? I want to be there to meet them and avoid a battle in Sol's system. Casualties could be unacceptable in that system. Any guesses?"

"Kier," Dr. Lin said.

"That's my guess, too," said Shear. "Militarily, it's perfect. At sixty-seven light-years from Earth it's only a few hours away, but Lock must know we'd pin him down to there. If we miss the guess, Mahat's forces could never handle the situation alone and I'd hate to have to retake Earth."

"I'm not basing my guess on a logical military situation," Lin said, "but on the emotional makeup of the man. He's arrogant enough. His arrogance has already cost him dearly near Lak and here."

Peer Shear pressed a button on his desk. "Send Dr. Heille in."

An elderly woman entered.

"Will you have a seat, madam?" Shear said and waited until the woman took a seat at the end of the conference table. He introduced everyone at the table.

"And to those of you who don't know her, she is Dr. Louise Heille, a psychiatrist originally from Svid but who has been practicing on Earth for the last thirty years," Shear said. "Stephen Lock approached her for treatment some fifteen years ago."

"He only came for the initial interview," she said. "We spoke for a few hours and he decided not to stay for treatment. That was understandable."

"Why didn't he stay?" asked Professor Lin.

"He was looking for an absolute truth. My science is not concerned with that kind of truth but with understanding of human nature. He found his truth with the Krits. Men who look for absolute truth rarely turn to psychotherapy. In Lock's case, he came to me to approve a preconceived notion, which was that I couldn't help him. Coming from an educated class, he had to be reassured personally that I couldn't help him. Psychiatry enjoys a good reputation among the educated. I get many such cases."

Shear said, "We are trying to guess the military moves this man might make. I've made available his personnel file when he was with the Earth Monitor Department and all that has been written about him."

She nodded. "Yes, and I've interviewed, at your request, many of his former acquaintances before leaving Earth."

"Would you call him arrogant?" Shear asked.

"No, anything but that. He is not arrogant, but very humble by a definition of humility the Krits would accept. For your purposes, you might consider him intelligent, fair in his dealings and completely convinced that he has the truth on his side. In his actions, he will be willful and do very well, limited only by his knowledge and rules of conduct."

Professor Lin said, "Doctor, this man has made at least two colossal blunders. Can you explain that?"

"It could be one of two things. The first is that he is not as intelligent as your planners . . ."

Shear shook his head. "No, that's not it. These were the kind of blunders I wouldn't expect from even the most naïve lieutenant. Every man knows enough not to stay in the open when a gun is being fired at him. Even if I were a better strategist than Lock, and I don't think I am, I would not have a fleet emerge within a few minutes of the defenders. It takes at least fifteen minutes to disconnect the pods. Only blind arrogance could make this possible."

"Perhaps he didn't plan it," said Dr. Heille. "The answer might be as simple as the fact that he may be dead and the Krits are keeping it secret. A member of the Krit hierarch could have the arrogance you speak of."

Shear nodded. "You said there were two possibilities."

"Yes, the second is that he's gone through another conversion."

"You mean returned to our side?"

"No." Dr. Heille said. "That would never happen. It is likely that he's converted within the Krit system of theology. His ego would never allow him to come back to the Confederation. If he decided that he was wrong, he would very likely take another view of the same theology. Krit theology can be very complex, and since it is a total system, many life-styles are represented in it."

"That makes sense," said Lin. "There is even one school, or heresy, in the theology, that calls for the agrarian life. It's not very popular at this time but it has a lot of strength with the intellectuals and a strong traditional support. The first Krits were farmers."

Shear was contemplative for a moment. "If something like that happened, they'd kill him?"

"Not necessarily," said Lin. "They may not know of his conversion. He might be sabotaging their whole operation in some way. Lock was a very subtle politician on Earth. I don't think a change of mind would be visible to the outside observer."

Dr. Heille said that she agreed. "In a group situation such as a command hierarchy, it is possible for a commander to give his ear to those he approves of and exclude the others. In case of failure, he can blame them. It has been done for a long time in military history. A man like Stephen Lock would have no trouble doing it."

"This all relies on the possibility that he changed his mind," said Elvuse. "Why should he?"

"Conversion cannot be rationally explained," Dr. Heille said. "It happens to every man at some point in his life. The most popular theory is that a multiple of frustrations will occasion a person to take an opposing viewpoint and convince himself that he really always had it. With men like Stephen Lock, it is hard to take such a simplistic view. Stephen Lock encountered no really major frustrations in his life."

"The more likely explanation," said Lin, "is that he was looking for an absolute truth, and rather than turning inward like most people, he turned outward to the Krits."

The discussion threatened to turn into a long debate which would have been enjoyed but which Shear saw as time-consuming when there was so little time to spare. He thanked Dr. Heille and politely dismissed her.

"The question remains," Shear said, "where will they assemble?"

"Kier," Lin repeated.

Elvuse asked, "Why don't they just meet at some arbitrary point deep in space that they may have agreed on previously? We'd never be able to guess."

Shear smiled. "The Ctz radical needs power from a sun or, as in the case of Kier, which is a solitary planet floating in deep space, the peculiar magnetic waves around it. The radical has to have a reference point. Have you ever heard of a ship emerging in deep space?"

Elvuse shrugged his shoulders.

Lin said, "Physics was never Arlin's strong point."

"I suppose that it's simply a question of my outguessing him," Shear said. "My instincts say Kier, so Kier is where we go."

"That's what they mean by command responsibility," Lin agreed. "Anyway, whether it's Lock or some other Krit, the religion has the weakness to think their God will protect them in the ultimate enterprise or that He may be angry at them by causing defeat, so they are likely to do the obvious. Religious folk, when you come down to it, can be predictable in many ways."

"You could both be wrong," Arlin Elvuse was quick to remind them.

"A calculated risk," Shear said. "We keep Mahat's fleet at Earth. If they assemble near Earth, we'll have a Keller warning and can be there in three hours. That'll be a severe disadvantage, but the prospect of meeting the Krit horde outside Sol's system makes the risk worthwhile."

A code was sent. It was an arbitrary number picked at random and designated an assembly point. For Kier, it was 467. The eight important commanders and subcommanders had it memorized. There was no way to break it since the computer used

Interlude Eleven: *Several Stories Arranged Under One Headline in The* SVID TRANSFAX
(interstellar edition)

TRIANGLE VICTOR AT KIER–KRITS ROUTED–
PEACE TALKS TO TAKE PLACE AT NICE

Commander Shear Lost in Vapor
Universe with 2,400

*Other Casualties Light for Triangle,
Heavy for Krits*

(All the following stories were on page one. They are arranged for comprehension rather than in order of importance.)

Oberland University—Kier was described by a spokesman for the Physics Department as an oddity of astronomy.

"It is a sunless planet existing some sixty-seven light-years from Earth with peculiar magnetic vibrations and pulsations," said Dr. Antroy Marimer, professor of astrophysics. "For reasons we have not fully understood, it is curiously regular in its pulsation without radiation variations. This makes it unusually easy to emerge from the vapor universes at any time. If Kier, itself, had an atmosphere other than methane and if it had surface temperatures within human range, it would be one of the more prosperous worlds in the Confederation. As it happens," the physicist continued, "it is beyond our abilities to transform it to our use and we have to be content to have a small chemical processing operation operated from orbit."

Asked about the battle, he said, "I'm not a military expert. All I can say is that it wasn't a drawn-out battle. Unlike solar systems, you can emerge at the second line of Kier. It must have all taken place in the space of hours. Naturally, I'm happy at its outcome."

- 30 -

Kier—Commander Peer Shear failed to emerge from the vapor universe before terminal time, according to a military commander on board the Second Wing out of Hobar.

What that means, stated Commander Josephus Arin of Lak, who assumed operational command of the battle, is that the control piloted by the veteran Hobarian captain cannot be recovered nor can any of its pods.

Twenty-four hundred persons were believed to have been aboard. An exact figure will be revealed as well as the names of those lost as soon as the military department has notified first of kin.

Commander Arin said, "This is a double tragedy. First Liennie passed on and now, her chief assistant at the Ib School."

Commander Arin was referring to the loss of one of the most important spiritual leaders of Hobar who died four weeks ago of bacteriological warfare. The Ib School is considered the most advanced of Hobar's Circle Schools. The loss to Hobar of both these individuals probably means the closing of the school, a governmental official on that planet said. He asked not to be named.

Du Shear and four daughters survive the commander.

(More on Shear's death on obituary page, inside.)

- 30 -

Oberland—Arlin Elvuse revealed today that biologist Dr. Margaret Moore was aboard the ill-fated ship under the command of Peer Shear.

The former Clown stated that he was responsible for her presence on board the vessel. At her request, he defied military authorities and arranged for her to be exchanged with an unnamed physician who did not want to go.

He said that she had wanted to be on hand when crew members of the Krit fleet out of allorg were interrogated. She wanted to determine what immediate steps could be taken to protect the remaining Allorg natives and to insure that the Allorg ban would be reinstated at any forthcoming peace talks.

He presented himself for arrest at the headquarters of the Triangle Forces. A spokesman for the security branch said that the matter would be taken up at a later date. He "technically" arrested Elvuse who remains free pending a resolution of the matter.

Arlin was reported to have taken residence at the home of Professor Jewette Lin and this evening declined further statements.

(More on Moore's death on obituary page, inside.)

- 30 -

by Masgor Lotter

Kier—(Aboard a fast fighter dubbed *Liennie VI* by its crew of two)—The Triangle Force, consisting of some eighty-seven controls and over three thousand fighter ships as pods, easily defeated a Krit force estimated to contain at least 20 per cent more ships, Wednesday (Confederation Standard Time).

We emerged at the second line and almost immediately came to action. The Krits were waiting for us.

The crew of the ship I was assigned to cover (the ship is easily representative of fighter-pods attached to the fleet) consisted of Captain Laveron Michaels of Hobar and John Atkins of Svid as backup pilot. "Lav," as she is called, was kind enough to turn on the radio shipwide so I could hear what they call "the chatter." ("Chatter" is the radio talk during battle.)

She did not have time to speak to me during the combat that lasted at least two hours, but prior to the battle and before we entered suspended animation while in orbit around Svid, we had a long discussion.

She had been a student at the Hobar Technical Institute and is not yet a full-fledged commerce pilot. She said that her title of Captain only applies when she is in actual command. Her Confederation fleet status is that of a sergeant-in-training. She wanted me to mention that over ninety pod-fighters have asked to be named *Liennie* after the recently fallen Circle mistress on

Hobar and that numbered designations had to be placed after each name.

There was no confusion since each ship is called by the pilot's name anyway.

John Atkins was a cargo-handler before the current war and said he can dock any ship of any size by "feel," that is, without instruments. As is the custom, when there was no real basis for determining who should be captain of any particular fighter, they asked for a random number from the computer on board. Women had even numbers and men had odd or some similar arrangement depending on the situation. Lav won since the computer put out an even number.

They both insisted that their experiences had been so different that there was no other basis of choice. Contrary to some notions, Hobarians did not have pre-eminence because of the planet of their birth. Only in the matter of faster-than-light travel can they claim pre-eminence.

I was told that as soon as we emerged at Kier, we would be awakened quickly and very probably be in immediate combat. We were given a drug just prior to suspended animation to insure that we would wake quickly. Lav warned that it would quicken our reaction time and that for intellectual activities it might affect our judgment.

She told me, in particular, that my journalistic activities might be compromised and that she had found it impossible to write anything for a few days after the drug was taken during the battle of Svid. I chose to take it and discover that I can sit here at the Keller type board and write anyway.

(Editor's Note: Much of this story had to be corrected by our copy editor. Reporter Lotter is normally accurate in her grammar; the drug apparently did affect her. She forgot the opening paragraph, for instance. It was added by a staff member. In view of her personal account of an unusual situation, however, we thought it best that except for grammatical and conventional journalistic corrections, it be left unchanged.)

The control that our fighter was attached to emerged and we were suddenly wide awake. It immediately jettisoned all pods in four directions which were random to prevent the plotting of courses by the enemy and was abandoned by its pilot who jumped into a waiting fighter. Our control was not immediately destroyed, which surprised us. We immediately went, with the sixteen other ships in our squadron, to destroy any Krit controls in the area. The idea was to prevent the Krits from proceeding to Earth.

We encountered no difficulty in breaking the guard around these controls since we were fighting as a unit and they were fighting individually. They seemed to have no training. Lav said that they were all probably new pilots and that the cream of their fleet had probably been massacred at Lak. She said that she didn't understand why the Krits hadn't distributed their finest pilots around to lead them.

Most of the Krit controls were destroyed within a half hour. There was no possibility that they would attack Earth now. Our forces had a great many backup controls still in the vapor universe.

About that time, we found out that Commander Peer Shear had not emerged from the vapor universe. Lav suggested that he was lost. An attempt to contact him by Keller from the second-in-command, Josephus Arin, proved fruitless and all were convinced that he had passed out of range in one of the multitude of vapor universes which the Keller was not programmed to reach.

(Editor's Note: Susequent to this dispatch, it was confirmed that Commander Shear and his party of 2,400 were lost. See separate story on page one.)

Our little fighter, a converted cargo handler, and the small squadron it was attached to, merged with other squadrons into a wing, and slowly, we began mopping up. Lav called it a slaughter. The Krits would not give up fighting until we had destroyed the lead ship containing the Krit Space Marshal; a sub-marshal then ordered his fleet to surrender. It is estimated that the Krits lost 60 per cent of their fleet at the Battle of Kier. Fortunately for them, they surrendered before the troop ships were destroyed.

Commander Arin ordered the Krits evacuated from the Krit troop-carrying pods and programmed those pods to dive into

Kier's raging atmosphere with all Allorg androids. Over 300,000 androids perished.

(Editor's Note: a subsequent check of the records captured from the Krits gives the figure at 345,797 androids.)

According to Arin, it is the order of the Triangle War Council that all Krit androids are to be destroyed.

Our own casualties were a little over a hundred ships (112 total, not including Shear's group, and 165 lives, again not including Shear's group—Ed.) and were considered light.

Our group will be leaving for Earth in a few minutes so I close this dispatch with a personal note. Let there be no more wars among us.

- 30 -

Nice, Earth—Peace talks are scheduled for three weeks hence to give the Krit delegation an opportunity to arrive.

According to Claymore Chase, who this day resumed his title of Representative since the House has officially been recalled, the issues that will be discussed will be the disposition of the planet Allorg, the reinstatement of the government of Rainbow's End, and the disposition of the governments of Krit and Mora's World. Minor issues will include the legal status of property seized by both sides during the period of the war, the disposition of prisoners, and criminal acts.

Rep. Chase declined to make public the details of the peace conference and the official position of the Confederation on these matters, saying that the proper place was at the conference table itself.

Expected to take part on behalf of the Krits will be Stephen Lock who was reported to be in control of the Krit government after a coup d'état.

Altaire of Svid and Chase are expected to be the principal negotiators for the Confederation. It was reported that the government of Hobar has delegated its interests at the conference to Altaire because of the apparent death of Peer Shear. Unconfirmed reports say that Commander Mahat is in disgrace and that her public appearance is only in the interest of presenting a solid front for the benefit of the Krits. Altaire was an attorney for the Pilot's Association, which is dominated by Hobarians and is well trusted by the government of that planet to take charge of their affairs until Hobar can replace May Mahat without public scandal.

The cause of Mahat's disgrace is believed to center around the fact that she is a hard-liner in the matter of peace terms while Hobar desires a return to normalcy without harshness.

Political observers have said that there is nothing more important on the minds of Rep. Chase and Ambassador Altaire than the disposition of the war in the quickest way possible and with the least bitterness possible.

The unresolved problem at the conference is Stephen Lock. No one is guessing what's on his mind, and his one big weapon, according to observers, is that he holds two Confederation planets and could prolong the war with over two million Allorgs known to have been transported to those two worlds and Krit. No one wants to fight the Krits on their home grounds.

- 30 -

CHAPTER TWELVE

TOWARD A LASTING PEACE

The limousine was quick on the major interchange at Nice. It was also unmarked.

Representative Claymore Chase had personally gone to the outport to pick up Altaire. Excluded from this diplomatic courtesy was Representative Mahat. She had to content herself with appearing at the official reception that night at the Hobarian Embassy.

"The advance party from Krit is already here," Chase told Altaire. "We've allowed them to reopen their embassy and naturally we're guarding it closely. They've made a lot of enemies among the population. The burning of the Congressional Library while the Kier battle was progressing was about the last outrage we could stand. They're making it very difficult for us to make a reasonable peace. There's talk in the capital of really unacceptable measures against them. And some hothead has actually challenged me from my district. I don't like the situation at all."

"But you will keep your promise to me to save them serious embarrassment?" Altaire asked.

"Yes, if I'm still in office. You know the politics of this planet as well as I do. It only takes ten per cent of the electorate in any district to call for a new election."

"We have a similar law," Altaire said, "but I'm not an elected official and my government has strong support for a return to normalcy. I have clear instructions about that."

"How I envy you," Chase sighed. "If only Earth had felt the

full brunt of this war, they'd feel the same way. As it happens, our casualties were too light for that. Very few felt it close to home. At the end of the war, slow-moving Earth has finally picked up the hate needed for the start of the war."

"You mustn't be so cynical, old friend. Things will work out. Earth isn't the only voice."

"It does have a powerful say," said Chase, "and the people are aware of it. I only hope I can keep the House of Representatives in order. Mahat's strong line is working against us. In the popular imagination, she represents Hobar. She's forming alliances among a good many Representatives and that's bad. I may have to challenge her on the floor."

"I think I have the solution to Mahat for you."

"You have my undivided attention, Mr. Ambassador."

"I'll contact Rass at the Technical Institute on Hobar and have him put Mahat on the hearing that will be looking into Peer Shear's death. She won't be able to refuse. No pilot can by tradition and Shear's importance will make it all that much more imperative that she attend. I think I can have Rass schedule it so that she'll have to depart very promptly."

Chase nodded.

"After she's left, I will get on the video and state what Hobar's position truly is. I am their Representative at these talks in all official matters."

"Good. With Hobar, which suffered the most casualties on our side, I can effectively silence the opposition. Of course, I'll retain Mahat as Speaker. Once she is defanged in this matter, she will be a most effective Speaker and it will save much of her pride."

"You're assuming Hobar will continue to elect her."

"They are practical to a fault and very forgiving. Besides, few men of stature on Hobar really care for politics. Anyway, if she is not elected, I can't be responsible and no one can accuse me of committing her political murder."

The reception at the Hobarian Embassy was formal and proper and there were no after-dinner conclaves in any of the numerous rooms that dotted the building. This was a sure indication that Mahat's influence was waning. No important person sought her views.

No one was more aware of it than Mahat. She was polite and cool to Chase, knowing that politically she had bitten off more than she could chew. Somehow she was sure that Chase had been responsible for the summons she had received that afternoon to take part in the hearing on Shear's death. She knew better than anyone present that it was a mere formality since he had been lost in the vapor universe and that any competent pilot could ask the formal questions and reach the obvious conclusions.

All she could do was to prepare for an early departure for Hobar the next morning.

So Mahat left. The sequence of events that would follow on Hobar in the next few weeks would insure that she would return to her seat but with vastly reduced powers. As Rass pointed out to the planetary Executive Council, her excessive powers were the result of poor communications until seven years ago. With the Keller system and fast ships, there was no longer any reason for a Representative to have such immense powers. However, a motion to reduce the term of Representatives was tabled in the interest of not embarrassing Mahat. When she was retired, it would again be considered. Though that motion was taken in Executive Session, it was arranged that Mahat find out about it. She took it as a warning, as was the intent of the planetary Executive Council.

She would drop from most controversial issues, leaving them to the Executive Council and take on the role of a business agent for Hobar, which was what Hobar wanted in their Representatives in the first place.

Stephen Lock arrived with some fanfare, largely to show that he didn't consider himself the loser in the war. He was met by Altaire, Chase, and Ambassador Lan Frate of Hobar at the outport. In a private room at the outport, everyone spoke pleasantries. Lock said that he regretted the burning of the library and offered to have Krit pay the expense of a new one. Chase politely declined.

Lock did bring up the delicate matter of freeing certain Krit collaborators and Chase said that all those who had not actually taken part in the insurrection had already been freed.

Casually, Lock said that a place for the insurrectionists might be found on Krit. The solution offered might be considered at the formal talks, Chase said. He knew that he would gladly accept the getting rid of these troublesome persons. But it was best that one's hand not be shown too soon.

The only really fruitful part of the meeting was the setting of a date for the beginning of the talks. A week was thought appropriate.

Altaire appeared on the video with Lan Frate to explain the Hobarian position. The interview had been carefully rehearsed with the able assistance of Representative Chase, who counted among his allies a very popular political commentator.

It did much to calm tempers.

Lan Frate, who understood his job as largely ceremonial, had a grand opportunity to show his pleasant style. The elderly man came on first to explain briefly the Hobarian philosophy of a peaceful life. He had the wisdom not to be lengthy with a video audience. He brought from his staff a mistress of the Circle, who calmly put holes in walls and bent steel. He chose her not only for her skill but for the similarity in her appearance to the Earthean concept of beauty. At the end of the demonstration, she brought out her three small children while Frate said, "Strength through calmness and peace." Frate repeated that phrase several times during the demonstration.

"Nice touch," said Chase to an assistant who was watching with him in the great man's private apartments.

"Sir?"

"I said 'nice touch.' You know, bringing out those children. We must not ignore this Frate fellow anymore. Jot a note to pirate him from the Hobarians for our little group. He's smart."

"Will he come?"

"My dear assistant, we don't ask him. We throw the fish to the Hobarian Executive Council. A few favors here and there do wonders."

"Yes, sir." The assistant was happy that his boss had lost his sour disposition of the past few days.

The camera focused in on Frate. "We, on Hobar, also believe in trust and so we have asked the experienced Altaire to watch our interests in the coming negotiations. He is more experienced at these things than I am."

The camera panned to Altaire. "There has been so much misunderstanding of late. Misunderstandings were what caused the war in which there are over two hundred thousand dead. No longer can we afford to allow such a situation to continue. We are going into the negotiations with a forgiving attitude and with the desire for a lasting peace. I speak for Svid and Hobar in this. We have known the worst in this war, so we speak with firsthand knowledge. . . ."

Chase watched approvingly as Altaire recited the speech he had written for him. Altaire had a good sense about him, thought Chase. He knew that it was Earth that had to be convinced and he had allowed Chase to have final say in the form of the speech.

"We should try to pirate him," Chase's assistant said.

"You must distinguish between a fine diplomatic technician with a decent personal philosophy like Frate and a true power like Altaire. Altaire will sit on the Board of Selectmen on Svid before the year is out. We can't steal the manpower that a planet really needs. We have to have ethics or we'll be out of office for certain. Be a good fellow and fix me a drink. I'm going to bed."

Stephen Lock also watched the broadcast. He knew that behind it was that master of political intrigue, Claymore Chase. It was good to be reminded how good Claymore Chase was at it. Without a word he poured himself another glass of wine while totally ignoring the sixteen-man embassy staff in the same room, drank it, and went to bed.

At length, the talks came. At one end of the rectangular table was Stephen Lock and two cronies who said nothing throughout the proceedings. At the other end was Claymore Chase, Altaire, and Lan Frate. Of the three, Lan Frate said absolutely nothing. He was back at his function of being ceremonial.

A man standing by the door said, "I, Peter Noles, GS-13

technician, certify that this room is whited; that there are no electronic devices of any kind and that all conversation held here will be free of unauthorized hearing." He left and closed the door behind him.

"May I compliment you on your efficiency, Representative Chase?" Lock said as an opener.

"Thank you. Shall we get down to business? We find no quarrel in your request that the peace treaty be written in Old English if permission is granted to translate it for the benefit of those ignorant of the tongue."

"It is granted," Lock said. "We will assist you, if you wish."

"That would be appreciated," Altaire said. As a lawyer, he could clearly see the value of such assistance. There would be no misunderstandings.

"We find no quarrel," continued Chase, "with your request that any version of the document known as the *Book* not be tampered with by any official or citizen of the Confederation. However, we deny the contention that this was ever the case. To simplify the matter, it can be a provision of the treaty that a perpetual copyright be granted the person holding the office of Chief Hierarch on Krit."

Stephen nodded. "We will let bygones be bygones in this matter and we will accept your simplification."

"The matters of the disposition of Mora's World and Rainbow's End need to be discussed further," finished Chase.

"Very well," said Stephen. "Of your requests, we will grant as you requested that we remove all personnel from the planet Allorg. We will swear an oath on the *Book* that this be done. You did not request this but it will bind us more than a treaty."

"That's most generous of you, sir," Chase said.

"As to the matter of exchanging of prisoners—we agree to all provisions in your request. It now becomes a matter of defining who is a prisoner."

"May I suggest, for simplification, of course," said Altaire, "that a prisoner is any person who does not wish to remain on either Confederation territory or Krit territory when the borders are drawn."

"I would except heretics from that definition," said Lock.

"And I would except any person guilty of murder by Confederation law," said Chase.

"That would include me," said Lock.

"Let us say 'all persons,'" suggested Altaire, who found himself in the role of arbitrator. "The copyright provision will protect Krit from unauthorized *Books*. We will enforce it, strictly."

Both men nodded.

"Your request that all Allorg androids be destroyed is granted without question," said Lock. "The process has begun. They are creatures of the Contrary. We will not interfere with your biologists' attempt to restore the natural Allorgs. They are God's creatures."

Chase was surprised at this sudden agreement. He thought that it would be an issue since the great part of Krit's army was android. Altaire wished Dr. Moore had been alive to see this. Neither man understood the theological subtleties by which Stephen Lock had arrived at this conclusion.

Good politician that he was, Lock was still a believer.

A number of minor items were also settled on the first day. The session was adjourned for the coming holidays.

The adjournment had been at the request of Stephen Lock. "Perhaps we should adjourn," he had said, "for this pagan 'spring holiday' of yours as an indication of our respect for your beliefs."

Chase smiled. "It has no religious significance as you well know. Perhaps you would like to use my African villa during the holidays to rest. As for us, we thank you for the breather. I'm getting old and I can use the rest."

Lock said, "We thank you for your offer but we will remain at Nice for the three-day holiday. We are happy that it will give you a time to rest."

In an adjoining room reserved for the Triangle negotiation team, Altaire asked, "What's he up to?"

"He's had to make a number of important concessions because of his religious beliefs. He doesn't want to be caught up in a roller coaster of concessions so he's going to keep us on the hot seat for a while. I was hoping he'd go to Africa out of the media's way. I suppose that now he'll romance them with his strong presence."

Lan Frate spoke up. "Sir, we have a number of documentary films espousing the way of life on Hobar and a new one on the bacteriological warfare on Hobar. It deals with the critical role played by an Earthman in saving Hobar from a more disastrous fate than it suffered. With your permission and co-operation, we might bring the effects of the war into Earth homes to remind the people that the Krits have not been very pleasant."

"What do you think, Altaire?"

"I'm inclined to think it will keep Lock from making any public appearances. It might also make him angry."

Chase nodded thoughtfully. "He came here with a plan; that's obvious from today's session. And that plan, whatever it is, does not concern itself with getting as much as he can but with setting up a postwar situation to his liking. So, he won't do anything to jeopardize it. Show the film."

Lan Frate nodded.

The film was even-toned and matter-of-fact. It documented the horrors of germ warfare almost without passion. It was believable.

Stephen Lock saw it that night in his quarters. He immediately canceled a press conference he had planned on calling the next day and chased his retinue from the room.

He got down on his knees. "Lord, thank you for showing me. I was in danger of greed and in danger of seeking glory. Let me not vary from your purpose. You have gifted Claymore Chase to counter my every move. Thank you for showing me. I remain your servant."

When the peace talks resumed three days later, the Triangle party was surprised to see an unsmiling Lock. They knew now that the talks would be over soon.

"Shall we talk of Rainbow's End today?" Altaire said.

Stephen Lock nodded.

"It must be returned to the Confederation and its government must be autonomous of Krit influence. It must be demilitarized."

"If it remains free of Confederation soldiers, it is agreed. We cannot have a hostile army so close to Krit."

Chase looked at Altaire and Frate. He was surprised at this sudden cave-in.

"Yes, it is agreed. We can both have a small mission of, say, fifty men each to insure the treaty," Chase said.

"That's acceptable," Lock said.

"So be it," Chase answered. "Now, as to Mora's World . . ."

"There will be no more polite fictions concerning Mora's World," said Lock. "It is close to Krit and has always been under our theocracy. It will be administered by Krit."

"Many citizens of Mora's World are non-Krits," said Altaire.

"Nine thousand four hundred and eighty-six are non-Krits by the last census," said Lock. "They will be evacuated to Rainbow's End."

"We cannot force anyone to leave his home," suggested Altaire.

"Those who do not leave will be killed by us. I am immovable on this question. Do you want to resume the war? This time, I will personally lead it."

Altaire said, "It is near lunch. Shall we resume afterward?"

Lock agreed to taking a two-hour break.

In their private conference room, Chase said to Altaire and Frate, "I'm going to scramble a call to Lin on Svid. We'll have to chance on it being decoded."

"It's unlikely to be picked up," said Altaire.

The elder statesman put through the call.

The professor had resumed civilian dress and appeared on the screen. Altaire explained the situation as it stood.

Lin didn't hesitate. "It seems our friend Alanis has made inroads into the mainstream of Krit thinking." He was talking about himself but he didn't need to specify the details of his forgery since both Altaire and Chase knew about it. "The Krits are going to go through a stage of agrarian simplicity. He's bluffing about Mora's World. He'll abandon it if he has to. But consider this: Should he die or be overthrown, his replacement as the power behind the throne might take issue with our control of a world that is predominantly Krit. Give it up, or better still, get something for it."

"What about the ten thousand non-Krits there?" asked Altaire.

Lin raised his arms. "You're not dealing with the civil rights of individuals in a court of law, Altaire. As distasteful as you may find it in your lawyer's heart, you are acting for two sovereign planets. Resettle them. That's the only advice I can give."

Altaire bowed his head and rubbed his forehead.

"I'll agree to it on the record," said Chase. "I'm used to backroom deals."

"I can't evade the responsibility," said Altaire.

"You most certainly can," said Chase, "and you will. I don't want you compromised. You will have to run the Insurance Act for us. I can't afford to have even a breath of scandal attached to your name. You agree with me, don't you, Jewette?"

"I do," the scholar said. "You're a public individual now, Altaire. You'll just have to play along."

"It's an outrage; it's a crime," Altaire said.

"It's also a necessity," Lin countered.

Altaire dropped into a chair. "All right."

"Representative, may I have a private word with Altaire?"

The politician nodded and walked out, followed by Frate.

"Are we alone?" Lin asked.

"Yes," said Altaire.

"Arlin Elvuse committed suicide this morning. He walked into a factory and entered a construction force field. A workman recognized him before he went in. We're keeping it quiet. Later, we'll announce that he died in an accident. We can't afford public scandal right now. I just wanted you to know."

Altaire nodded. He was getting used to bad news. "Do you know why he did it?"

Lin said, "He didn't leave a note but I can guess. It was Dr. Moore's death that did it. He felt responsible."

"It's hard to imagine Elvuse feeling responsible about anything," Altaire said with a sad smile.

Lin nodded, smiling with equal sadness. "We must think of it as his final irreverence."

The circuit was closed.

Altaire returned to the peace conference on an empty stomach. He listened to Chase sell out Mora's World. He demanded that hard currency be given to each displaced person for the value of his property. Lock agreed. He was getting a planet cheap.

Altaire offered, in a businesslike manner, since his heart had left the negotiations, to make Krit part of the Insurance Act. It was refused outright. Altaire was relieved.

It was agreed instead that a ministerial-level conference would be held on property matters and that its agreements would have the force of the treaty.

Lock also announced, at the close of the negotiations, that Krit would no longer be part of the Confederation. Within a year, it would leave the all-important Credit Committee at Nice and, except for its own needs, would give up all pilots. Within ten years, it expected to give up all commerce with the Confederation.

"At least they won't be a threat to us in our lifetime or in that of our children," Chase said afterward. "They're giving up their industrial base."

Altaire only nodded.

"You seem upset by the whole thing. Surely you didn't think we'd have everything our own way. Why don't you come down to my villa with me while the legal technicians put our words into that silly jargon of theirs? The vacation will do you good." Chase wrapped his arms around Altaire and Frate and led them down the hall.

Postscript: The Shoes

The death toll from the bacteriological attack on Hobar had crept up to 52,456 in the second year (local) after the war. The original organisms had largely died out but certain strains had mutated to survive in Hobar's harsh environment.

One strain had even claimed the lives of eighteen Svids when it accidentally traveled to that planet by ship in spite of stringent measures and detoxification efforts. This had moved numerous microbiologists from Svid to volunteer their efforts to help Hobar wipe out the remaining organisms.

Many nonprofessional technicians with some background in chemistry had also gone to Hobar.

The conclusion, at the end of the second year, could be stated on a curve. Deaths, the first month after the initial attack that had claimed 39,876 lives, were a whopping 4,856. During the same month two years later, deaths had dropped to 8. The bacteria were falling victim to natural enemies.

The team of Svids who had come to help was preparing to go home minus sixteen of their own numbers who had fallen victim to the bug.

But first, readings would be taken at various parts of Hobar to make sure. The tests, now well developed after two years, were foolproof.

So it was that two technicians from Svid accompanied a Hobarian guide to the Village of Ib for some final readings. They were setting up their equipment on the outskirts of the village when a woman walked past them a few yards away.

The Hobarian guide bowed slightly, putting his right fist into his left hand. The greeting was returned.

One of the Svids asked, "Who is that?"

The Hobarian smiled. "Mistress Du of the Ib Circle School."

The name didn't register with the technician, who had come to Hobar only two months previously as one of the last volunteers.

"You've heard of Mistress Liennie?"

The Svid nodded.

"She's her adopted daughter. She was born on Krit and no one ever thought that she would become a Mistress of the Circle. When Liennie died in the attack and her chief deputy, Peer Shear, died in the vapor universe, we all thought that the Ib School would close. You have to understand. Some schools, like the Albert School, are institutions. They pass from one master to the next, but schools like the Ib School only survive if the masters are special. These small schools are the best. No one would have imagined that Du would become a Mistress of the Circle. We all forgot the important things. She was competent and had been under the influence of Liennie for over twenty-two years. What we remembered, to our shame, was that she had come from Krit.

"But she went to the leading schools and let the masters judge. Without exception, they pronounced her competent."

The technician admitted that this didn't make much sense to him and the guide promised to take him to the Ib School for a demonstration of the Circle after they had finished their work.

They watched Mistress Du walk to a small power glider that had just landed. She had a sack attached to her belt.

The pilot was a fifteen-(standard)-year-old boy. He gave the greeting and helped Du strap in. She handed him a piece of paper and asked to be taken to the co-ordinates that had been written out for her.

"Can we get there, spend an hour, and return before the evening storms?"

"Yes, mistress," said the young man. "It'll be no trouble."

"You will be sure to thank your father for allowing me to use his aircraft."

He nodded and set the glider in motion.

She found it a glorious flight. She always enjoyed flying in a small aircraft without artificial gravity. Two hours later, they landed.

"What is this place, mistress?" he asked, looking at buildings, now in ruin.

"It once was the Krit Embassy. They are no longer welcome on this world," she said. "Will you wait here, please?"

She walked past a large force field pole, which was now tipped over uselessly, and made her way to the square of the embassy.

In front of the temple, she dug a hole with a small energy weapon and took from her sack a pair of slippers which once had belonged to Liennie and a heavy pair of space boots which Commander Rone had taken from his feet when Du had explained what she intended to do.

"It will be my honor to allow you to use my boots in place of your husband's. He became a dear friend in the short time I knew him."

"That's why I asked you," she had told him simply.

What she had explained to Rone was that it was an ancient custom on Krit to bury the shoes of departed family members two years after they had passed from mortal existence. It was a good custom she had explained, and Rone had readily agreed.

So Du buried the slippers and boots side by side and sat in meditation for a time.